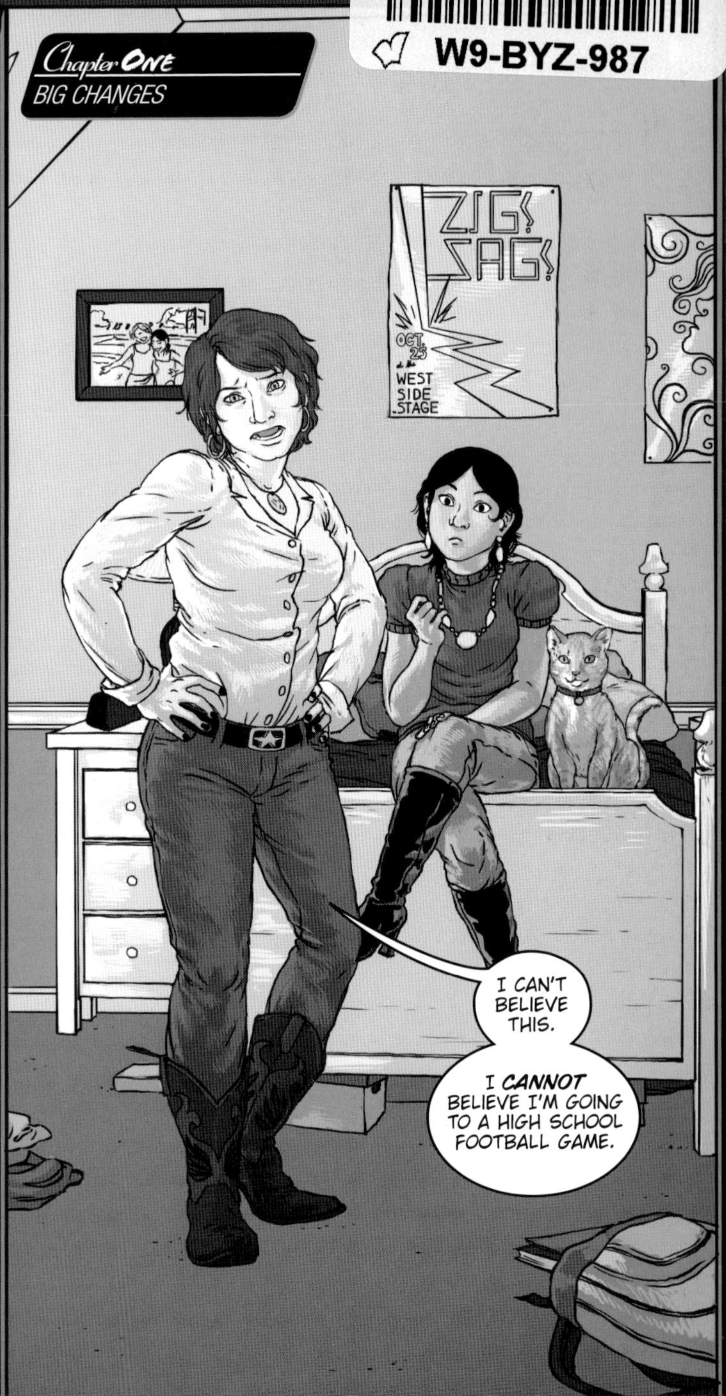
Chapter One
BIG CHANGES
OCT. 25
WEST SIDE STAGE
I CAN'T BELIEVE THIS.
I *CANNOT* BELIEVE I'M GOING TO A HIGH SCHOOL FOOTBALL GAME.

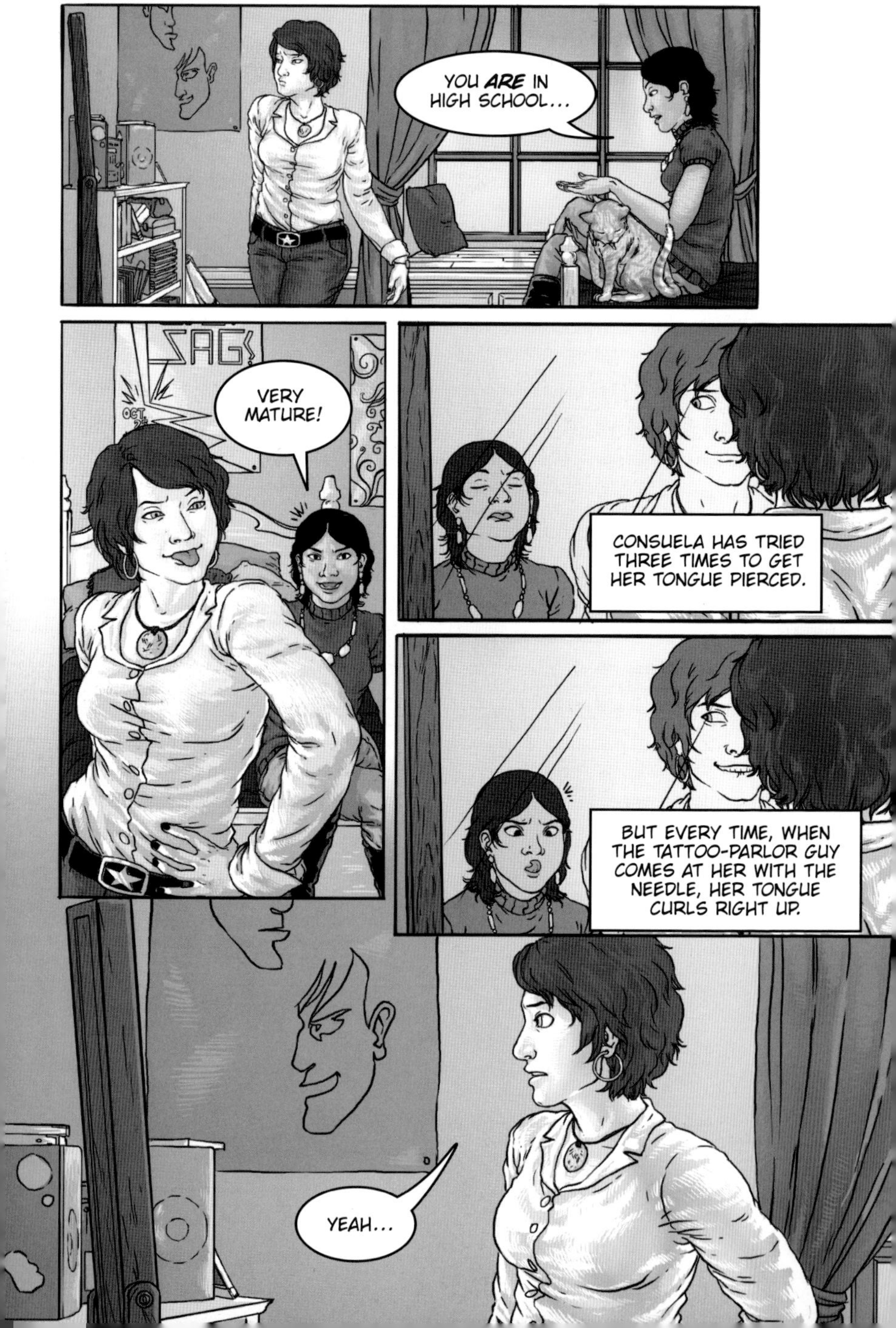
YOU ARE IN HIGH SCHOOL...
VERY MATURE!
CONSUELA HAS TRIED THREE TIMES TO GET HER TONGUE PIERCED.
BUT EVERY TIME, WHEN THE TATTOO-PARLOR GUY COMES AT HER WITH THE NEEDLE, HER TONGUE CURLS RIGHT UP.
YEAH...

MY BOYFRIEND IS A MONSTER

He Loves Me, He Loves Me Not

OR
DOUBLE DATE

OR
TWO OF A KIND

OR
OPPOSITES ATTRACT

OR
A REAL LOVE-HATE RELATIONSHIP

OR
TWO'S COMPANY, THREE'S A CROWD

OR
YOU CAN'T JUDGE A JOCK BY HIS COVER

OR
HAVEN'T I SEEN YOU SOMEPLACE BEFORE?

ROBIN MAYHALL

Illustrated by KRISTEN CELLA

with additional illustrations by JANE IRWIN, DIRK TIEDE, and JENN MANLEY LEE

GRAPHIC UNIVERSE™ · MINNEAPOLIS

STORY BY
ROBIN MAYHALL
ILLUSTRATIONS BY
KRISTEN CELLA

WITH ADDITIONAL ILLUSTRATIONS BY
JANE IRWIN, DIRK TIEDE, AND JENN MANLEY LEE
ARTIST'S LAB ASSISTANTS
MO OH AND ALEX VALLEAU

LETTERING BY
ZACK GIALLONGO AND GRACE LU
COVER COLORING BY
JENN MANLEY LEE

Copyright © 2013 by Lerner Publishing Group, Inc.

Graphic Universe™ is a trademark of Lerner Publishing Group, Inc.

Graphic Universe™
A division of Lerner Publishing Group, Inc.
241 First Avenue North
Minneapolis, MN 55401 U.S.A.

Website address: www.lernerbooks.com

Main body text set in CCWildwords. Typeface provided by Comicraft Design.

Library of Congress Cataloging-in-Publication Data

Mayhall, Robin.
    He loves me, he loves me not / by Robin Mayhall ; illustrated by Kristen Cella with additional illustrations by Jane Irwin and Dirk Tiede.
    p. cm. — (My boyfriend is a monster ; #07)
    Summary: Upon moving to small-town Texas partway into her junior year of high school, Serena sees parallels between the novel her class is studying, Dr. Jekyll and Mr. Hyde, and the two men in her life: boyfriend Lance, the quarterback, and outsider Cam.
    ISBN 978–0–7613–6005–6 (lib. bdg. : alk. paper)
    1. Graphic novels. [1. Graphic novels. 2. High schools—Fiction. 3. Schools—Fiction. 4. Dating (Social customs)—Fiction. 5. Moving, Household—Fiction. 6. Family life—Texas—Fiction. 7. Texas—Fiction. 8. Horror stories.] I. Cella, Kristen, ill. II. Title.
PZ7.7.M39He 2013
741.5'973—dc23   2011044491

Manufactured in the United States of America
1 – PP – 12/31/12

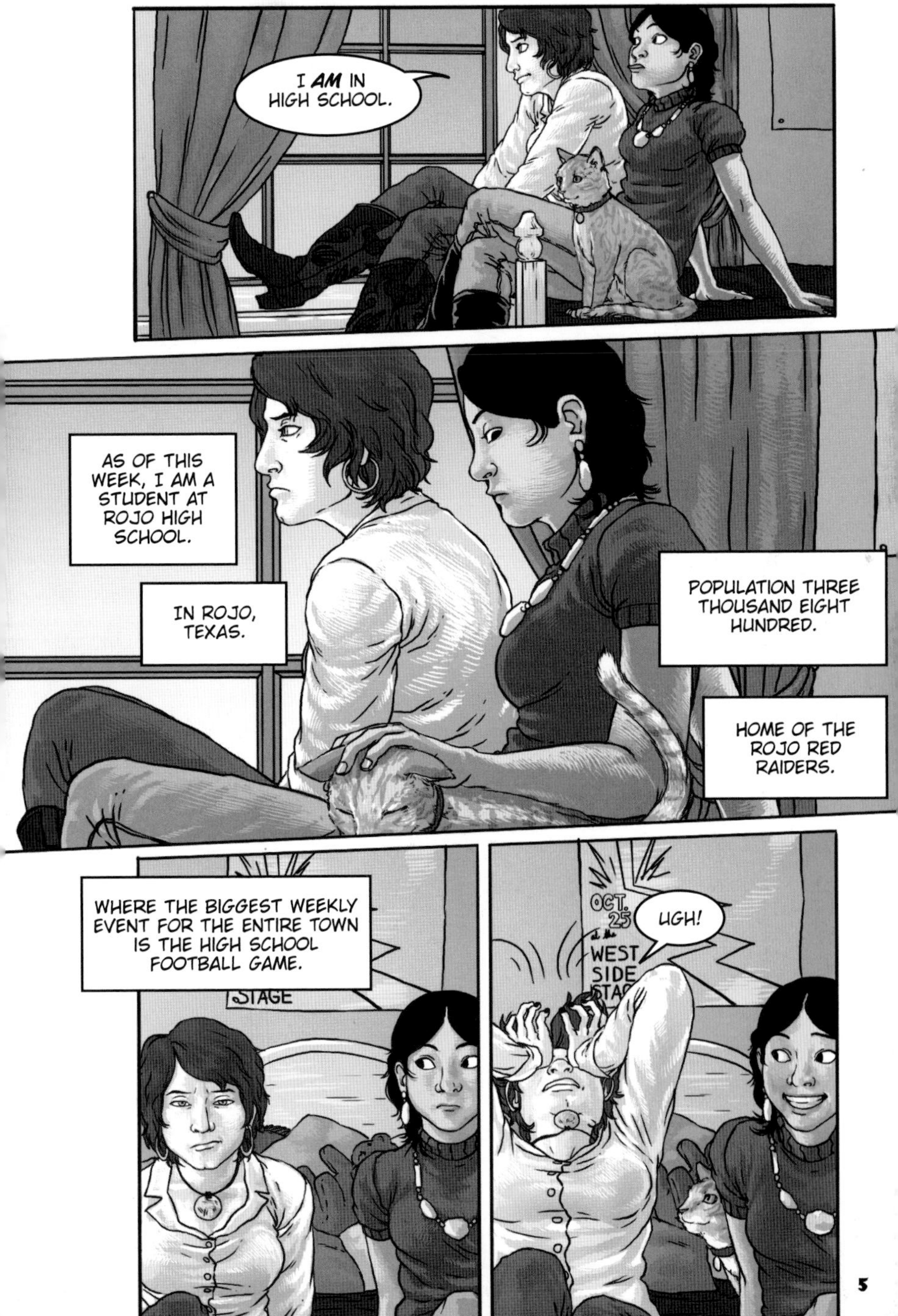
I *AM* IN HIGH SCHOOL.
AS OF THIS WEEK, I AM A STUDENT AT ROJO HIGH SCHOOL.
IN ROJO, TEXAS.
POPULATION THREE THOUSAND EIGHT HUNDRED.
HOME OF THE ROJO RED RAIDERS.
WHERE THE BIGGEST WEEKLY EVENT FOR THE ENTIRE TOWN IS THE HIGH SCHOOL FOOTBALL GAME.
STAGE
OCT. 25
WEST
SIDE
UGH!

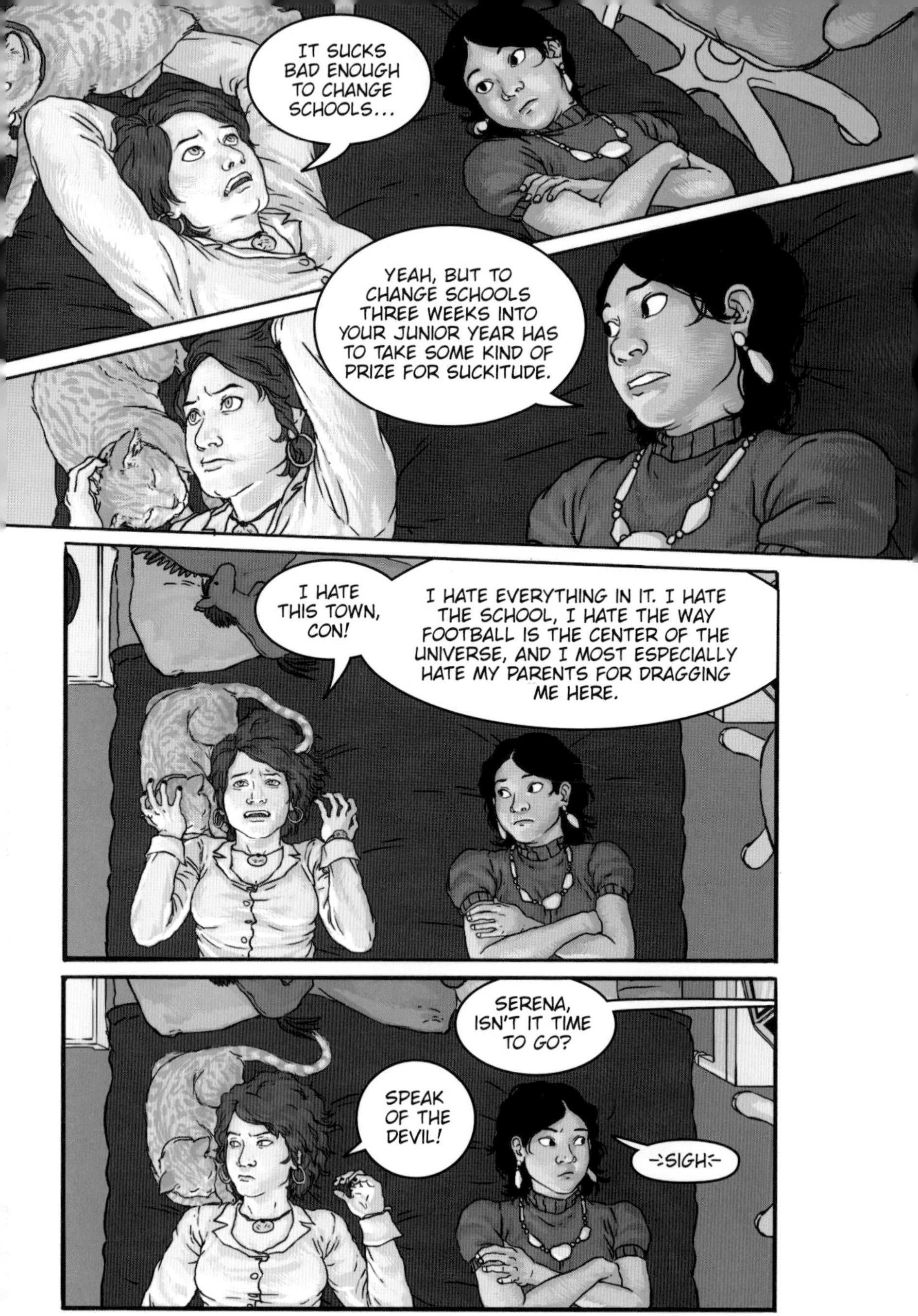
IT SUCKS BAD ENOUGH TO CHANGE SCHOOLS...
YEAH, BUT TO CHANGE SCHOOLS THREE WEEKS INTO YOUR JUNIOR YEAR HAS TO TAKE SOME KIND OF PRIZE FOR SUCKITUDE.
I HATE THIS TOWN, CON!
I HATE EVERYTHING IN IT. I HATE THE SCHOOL, I HATE THE WAY FOOTBALL IS THE CENTER OF THE UNIVERSE, AND I MOST ESPECIALLY HATE MY PARENTS FOR DRAGGING ME HERE.
SERENA, ISN'T IT TIME TO GO?
SPEAK OF THE DEVIL!
-SIGH-

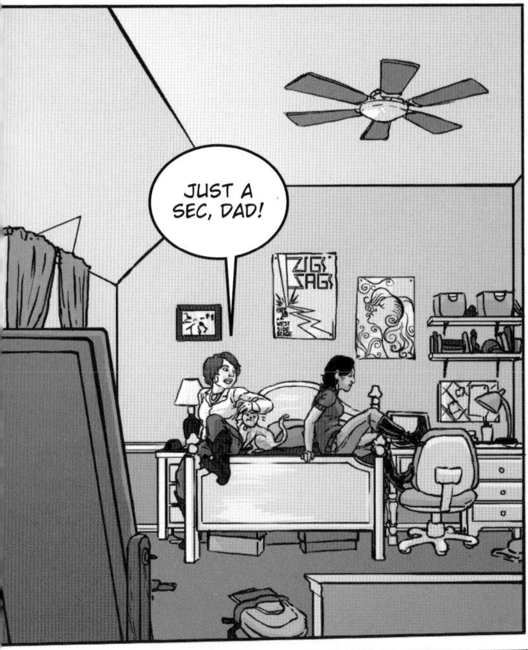
JUST A SEC, DAD!
ZIG SAG

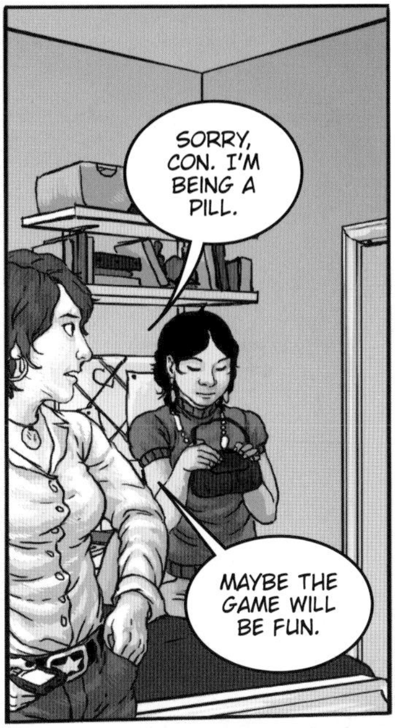
SORRY, CON. I'M BEING A PILL.
MAYBE THE GAME WILL BE FUN.

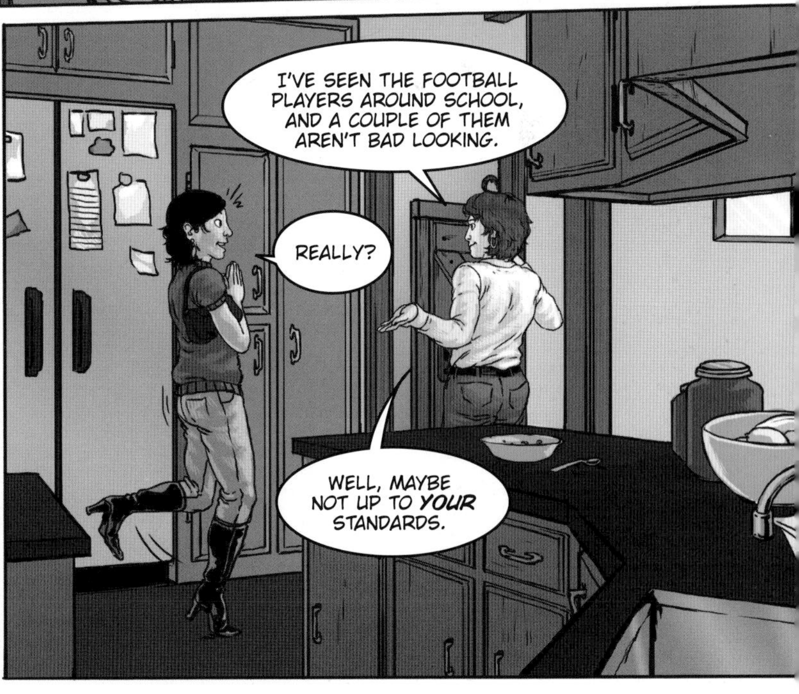
I'VE SEEN THE FOOTBALL PLAYERS AROUND SCHOOL, AND A COUPLE OF THEM AREN'T BAD LOOKING.
REALLY?
WELL, MAYBE NOT UP TO ***YOUR*** STANDARDS.

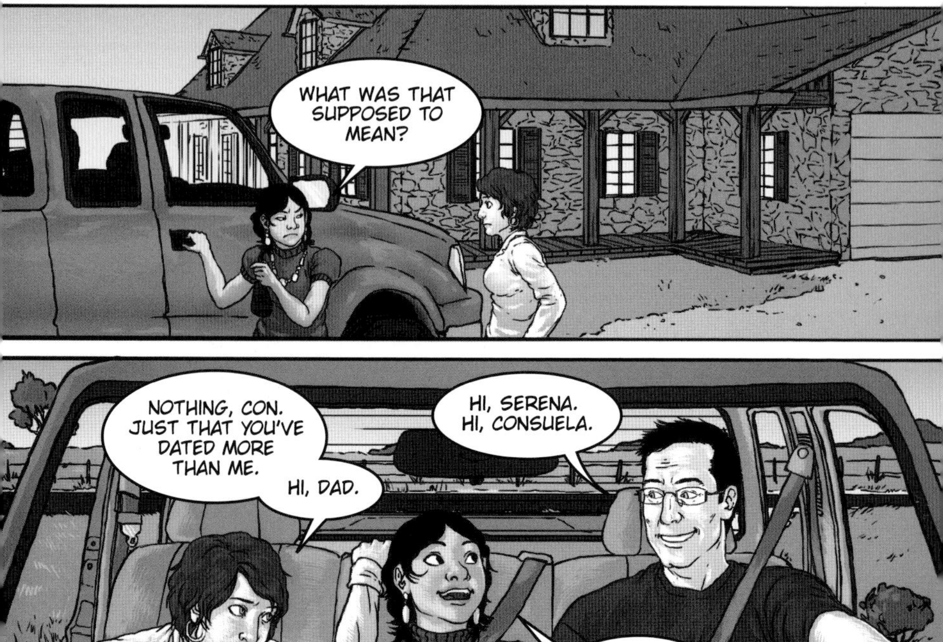
WHAT WAS THAT SUPPOSED TO MEAN?
NOTHING, CON. JUST THAT YOU'VE DATED MORE THAN ME.
HI, DAD.
HI, SERENA. HI, CONSUELA.
HI, MR. BOB. THANKS FOR DRIVING US TO THE GAME.
NO PROBLEM. I'M GLAD YOU CONVINCED SERENA TO GO.
DAD...
I JUST WANT YOU TO GET OUT MORE, HONEY, AND MEET SOME NEW FRIENDS HERE.
NO OFFENSE, OF COURSE, CONNIE.

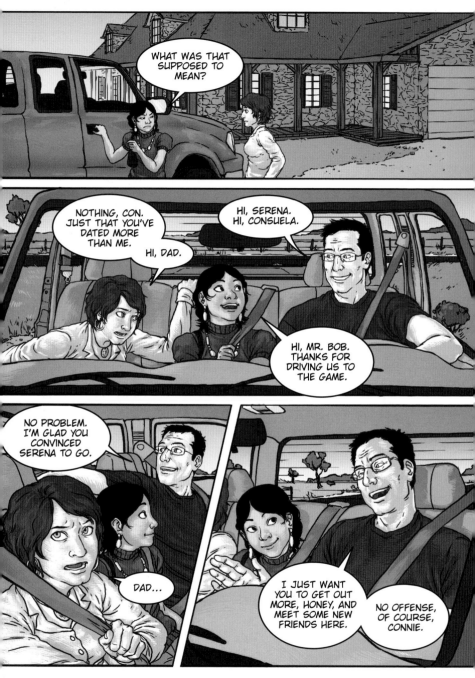

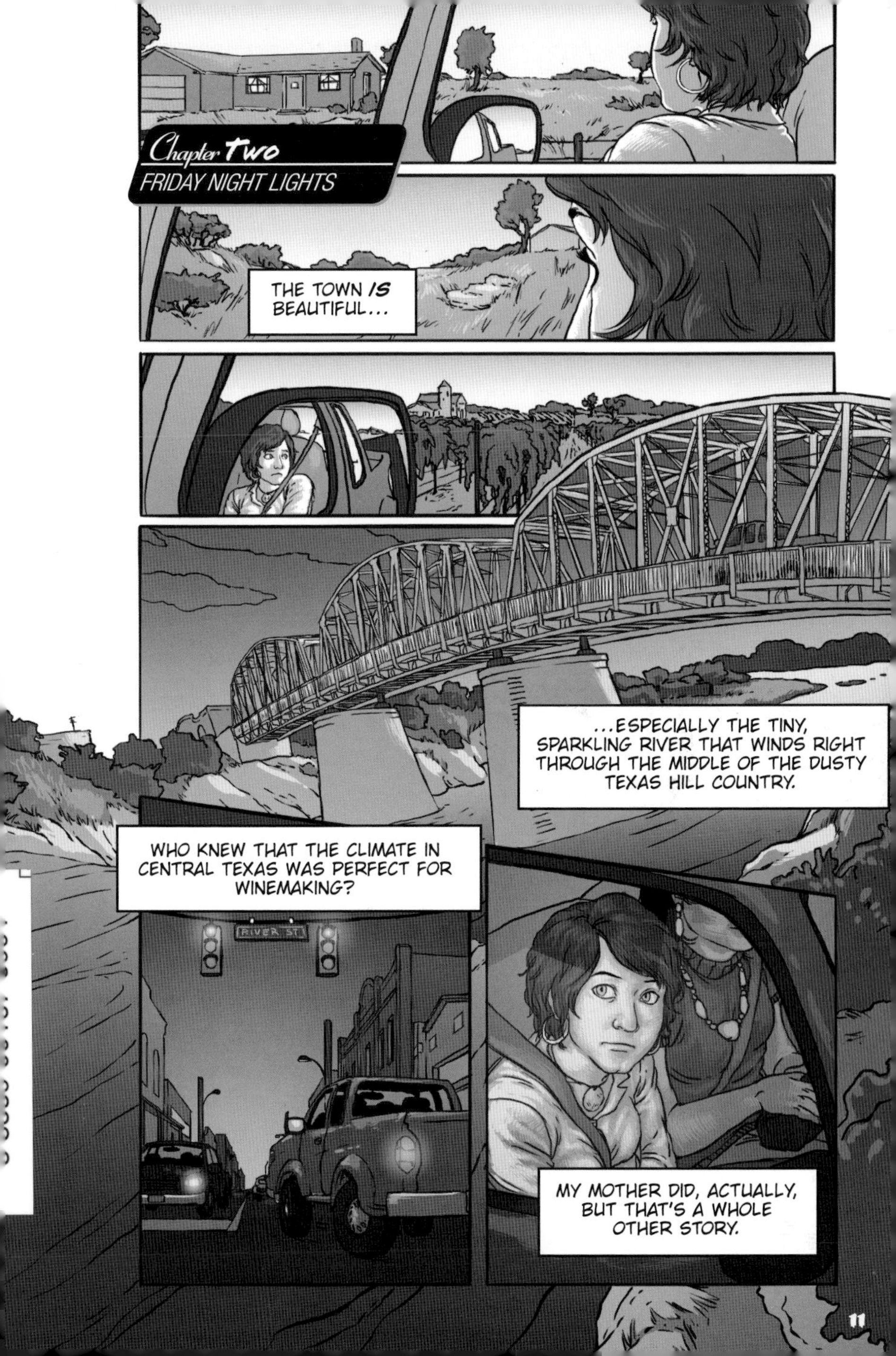
Chapter Two
FRIDAY NIGHT LIGHTS
THE TOWN *IS* BEAUTIFUL...
...ESPECIALLY THE TINY, SPARKLING RIVER THAT WINDS RIGHT THROUGH THE MIDDLE OF THE DUSTY TEXAS HILL COUNTRY.
WHO KNEW THAT THE CLIMATE IN CENTRAL TEXAS WAS PERFECT FOR WINEMAKING?
RIVER ST
MY MOTHER DID, ACTUALLY, BUT THAT'S A WHOLE OTHER STORY.

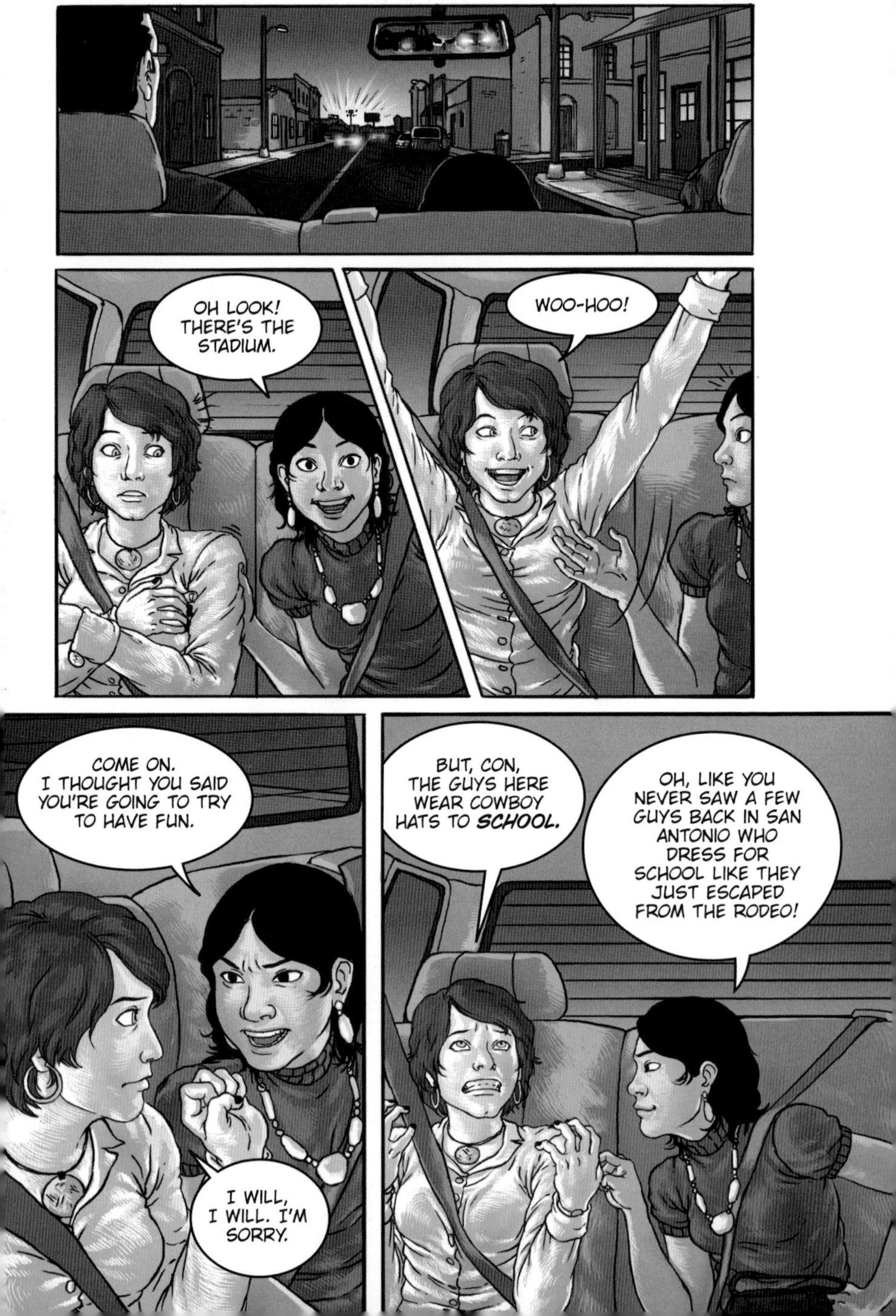
OH LOOK! THERE'S THE STADIUM.
WOO-HOO!
COME ON. I THOUGHT YOU SAID YOU'RE GOING TO TRY TO HAVE FUN.
I WILL, I WILL. I'M SORRY.
BUT, CON, THE GUYS HERE WEAR COWBOY HATS TO *SCHOOL.*
OH, LIKE YOU NEVER SAW A FEW GUYS BACK IN SAN ANTONIO WHO DRESS FOR SCHOOL LIKE THEY JUST ESCAPED FROM THE RODEO!

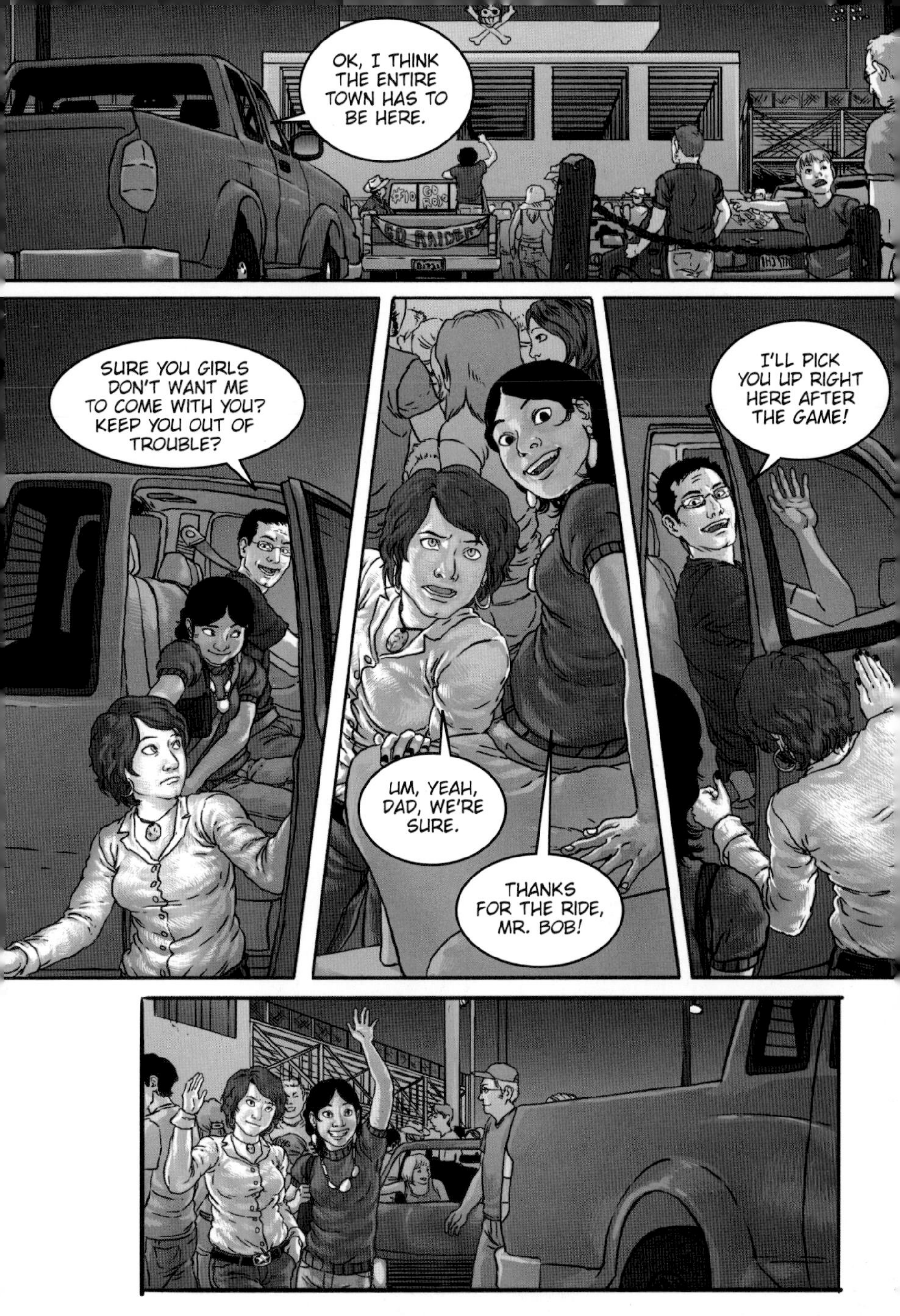
OK, I THINK THE ENTIRE TOWN HAS TO BE HERE.
#10 GO ROJO
GO RAIDERS
SURE YOU GIRLS DON'T WANT ME TO COME WITH YOU? KEEP YOU OUT OF TROUBLE?
UM, YEAH, DAD, WE'RE SURE.
THANKS FOR THE RIDE, MR. BOB!
I'LL PICK YOU UP RIGHT HERE AFTER THE GAME!

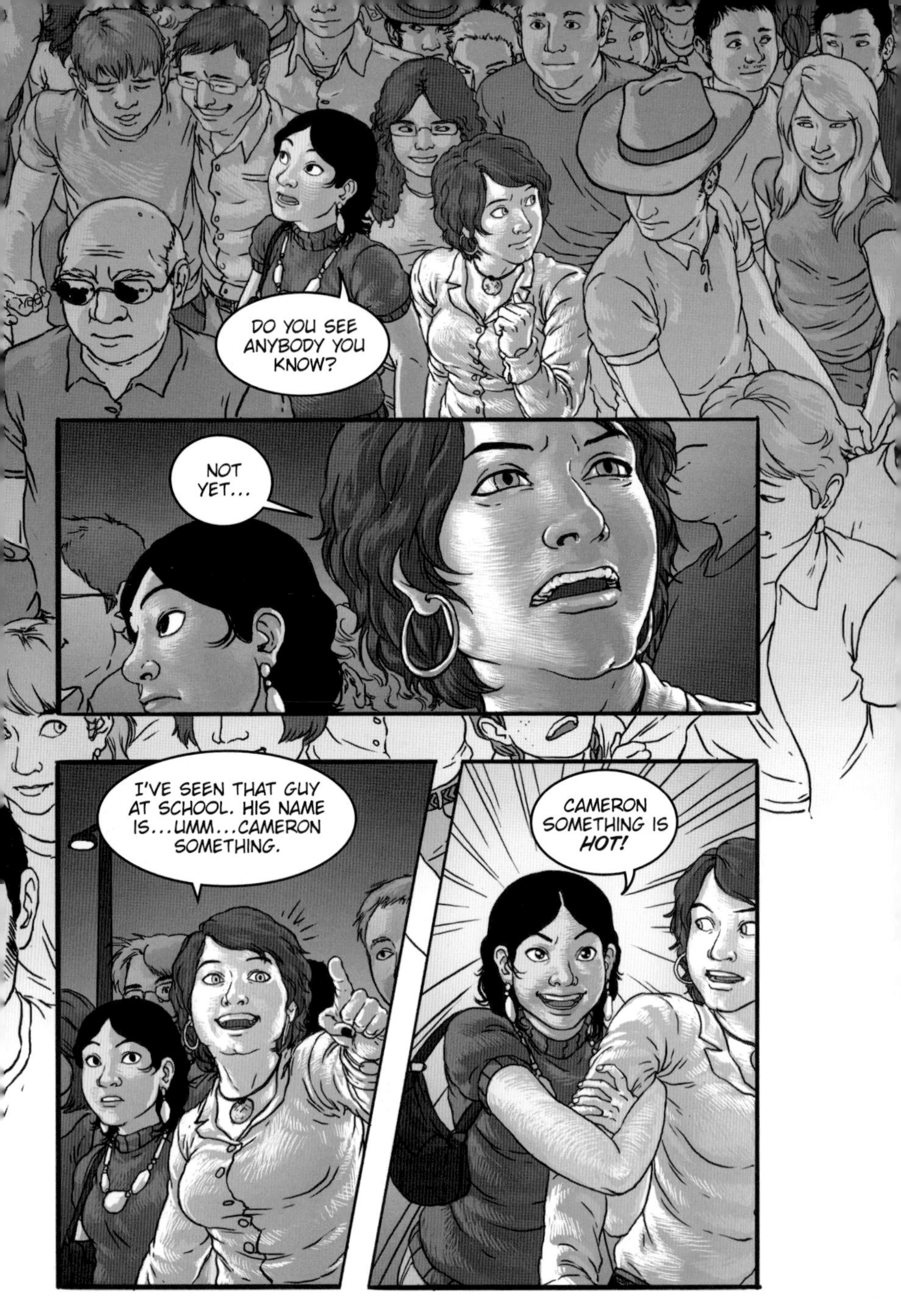
DO YOU SEE ANYBODY YOU KNOW?
NOT YET...
I'VE SEEN THAT GUY AT SCHOOL. HIS NAME IS...UMM...CAMERON SOMETHING.
CAMERON SOMETHING IS ***HOT!***

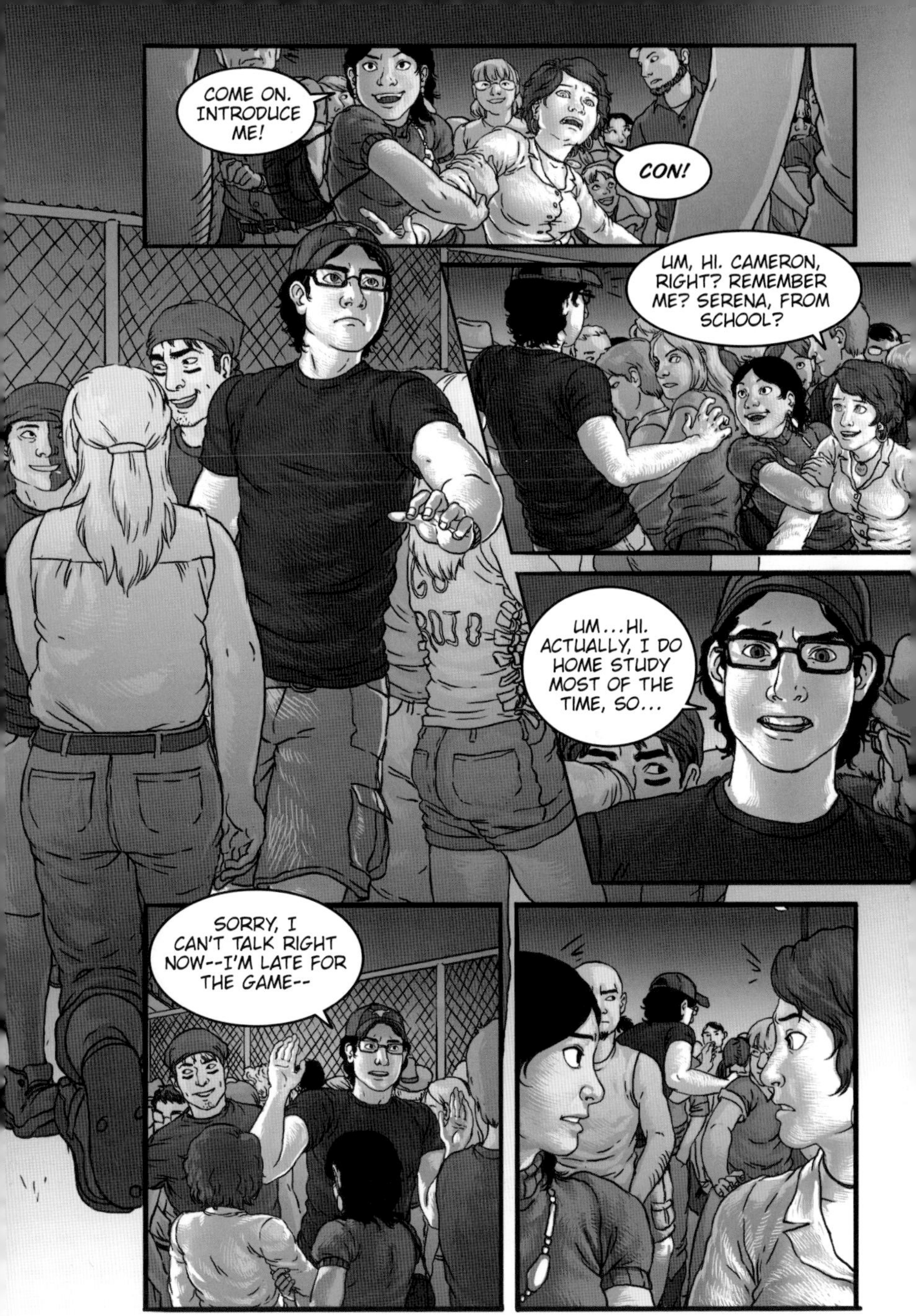
COME ON. INTRODUCE ME!
CON!
UM, HI. CAMERON, RIGHT? REMEMBER ME? SERENA, FROM SCHOOL?
GO ROJO
UM...HI. ACTUALLY, I DO HOME STUDY MOST OF THE TIME, SO...
SORRY, I CAN'T TALK RIGHT NOW--I'M LATE FOR THE GAME--

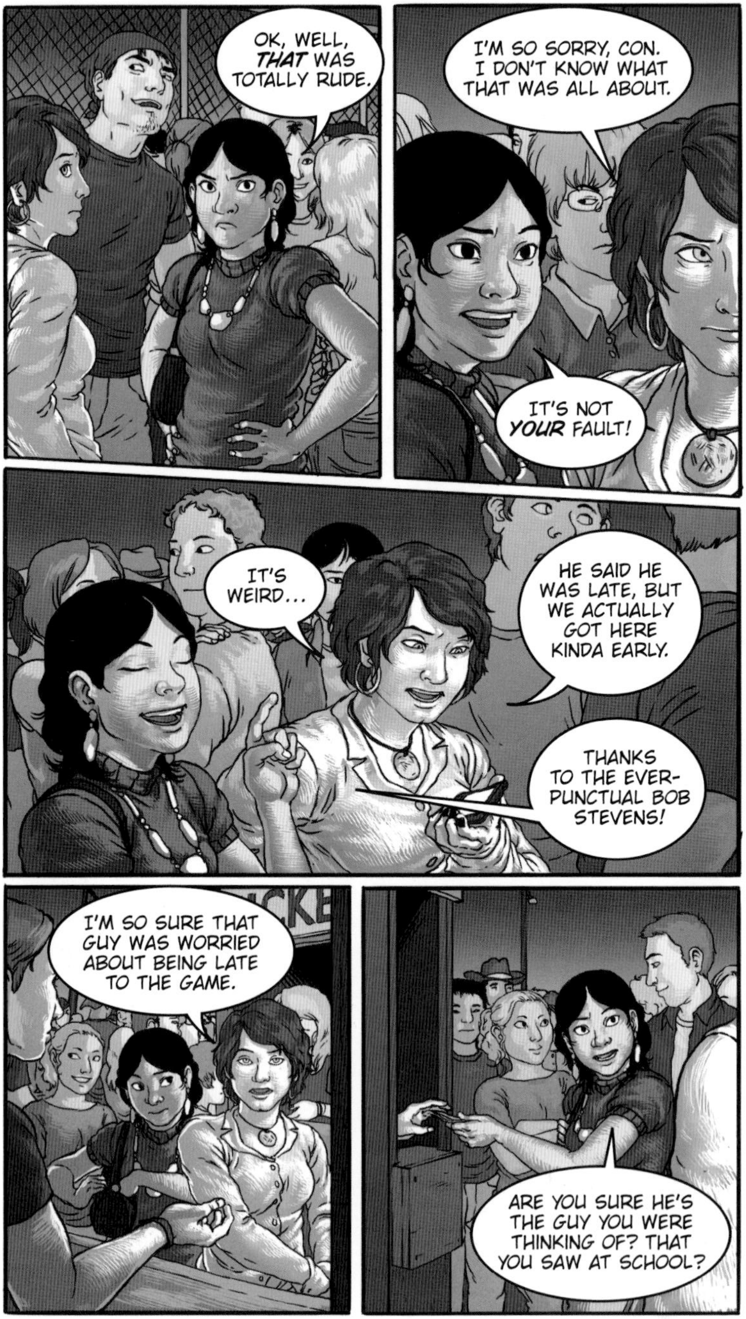
OK, WELL, *THAT* WAS TOTALLY RUDE.
I'M SO SORRY, CON. I DON'T KNOW WHAT THAT WAS ALL ABOUT.
IT'S NOT *YOUR* FAULT!
IT'S WEIRD...
HE SAID HE WAS LATE, BUT WE ACTUALLY GOT HERE KINDA EARLY.
THANKS TO THE EVER-PUNCTUAL BOB STEVENS!
I'M SO SURE THAT GUY WAS WORRIED ABOUT BEING LATE TO THE GAME.
ARE YOU SURE HE'S THE GUY YOU WERE THINKING OF? THAT YOU SAW AT SCHOOL?

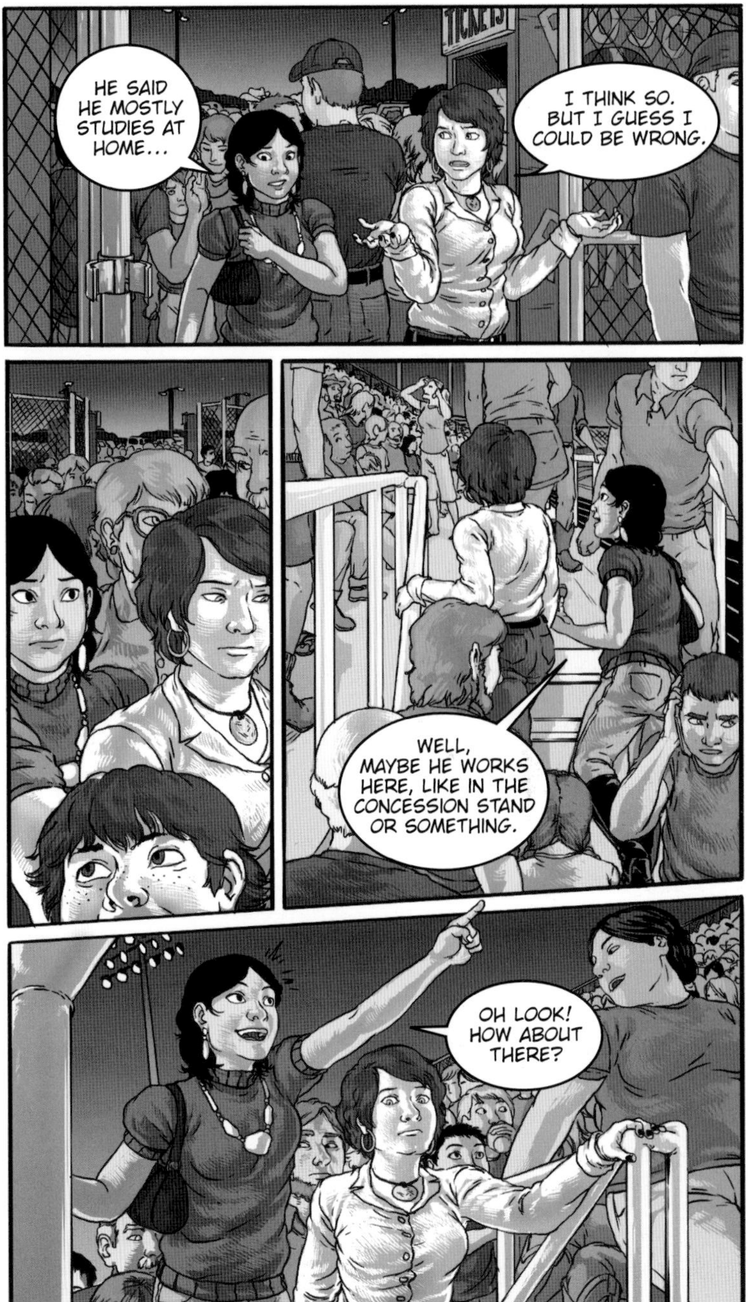
HE SAID HE MOSTLY STUDIES AT HOME...
I THINK SO. BUT I GUESS I COULD BE WRONG.
WELL, MAYBE HE WORKS HERE, LIKE IN THE CONCESSION STAND OR SOMETHING.
OH LOOK! HOW ABOUT THERE?

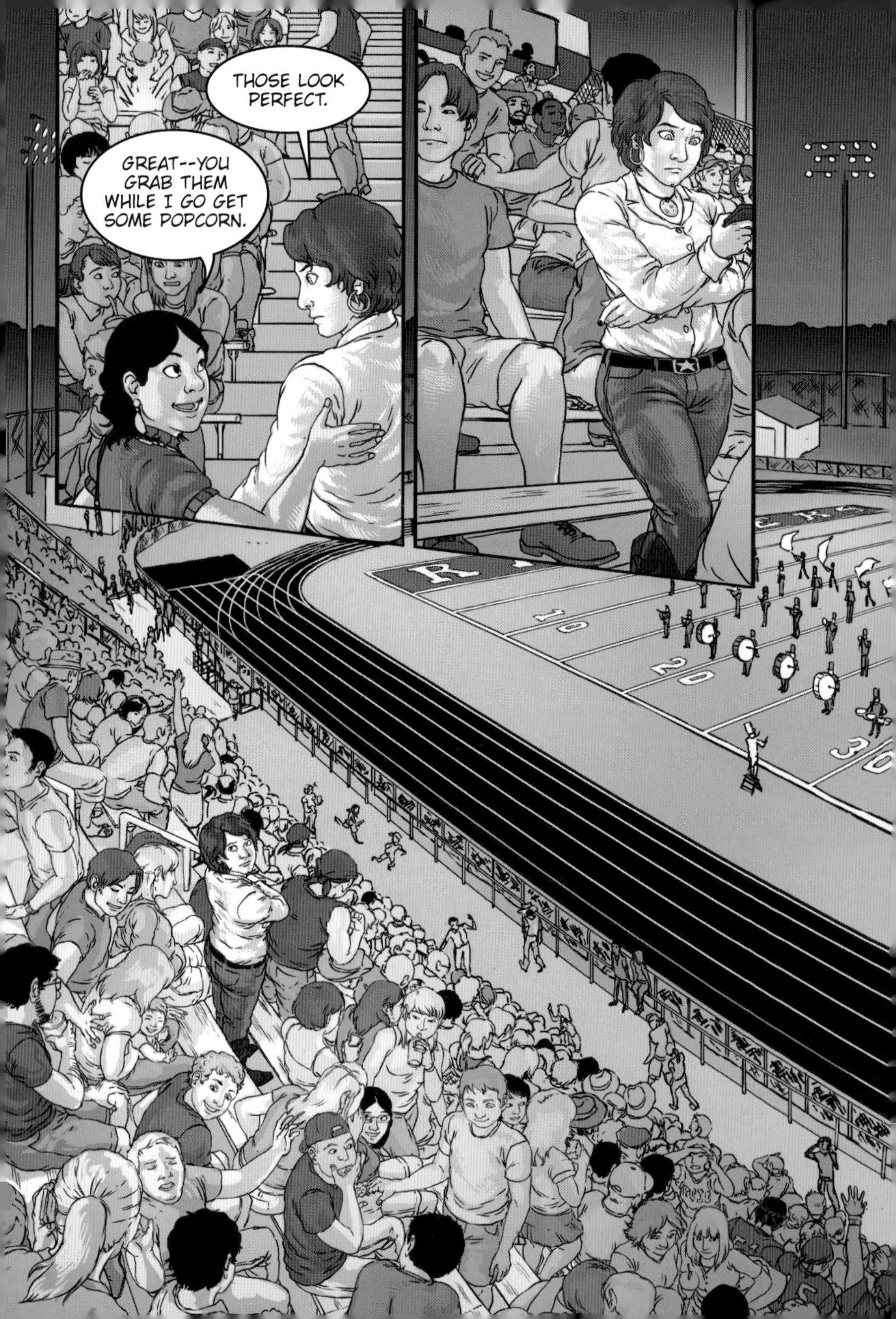
THOSE LOOK PERFECT.
GREAT--YOU GRAB THEM WHILE I GO GET SOME POPCORN.

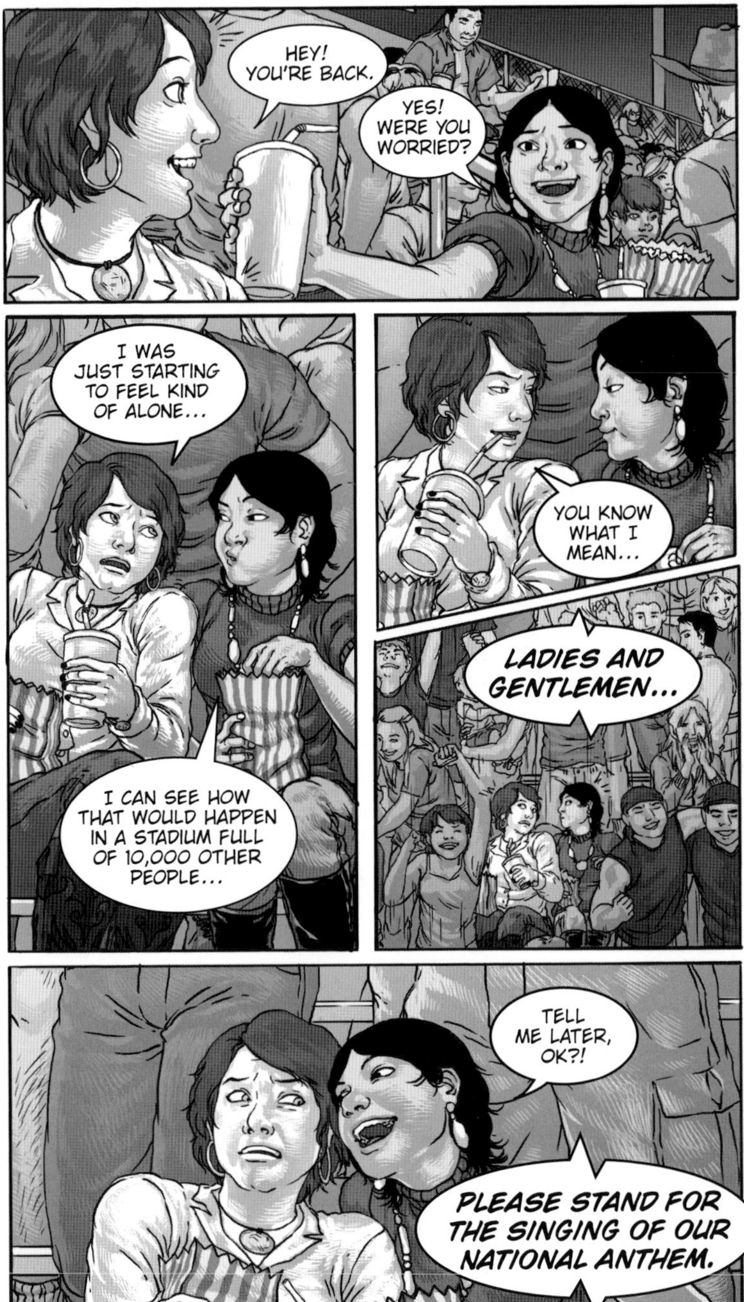
HEY! YOU'RE BACK.
YES! WERE YOU WORRIED?
I WAS JUST STARTING TO FEEL KIND OF ALONE...
I CAN SEE HOW THAT WOULD HAPPEN IN A STADIUM FULL OF 10,000 OTHER PEOPLE...
YOU KNOW WHAT I MEAN...
LADIES AND GENTLEMEN...
TELL ME LATER, OK?!
PLEASE STAND FOR THE SINGING OF OUR NATIONAL ANTHEM.

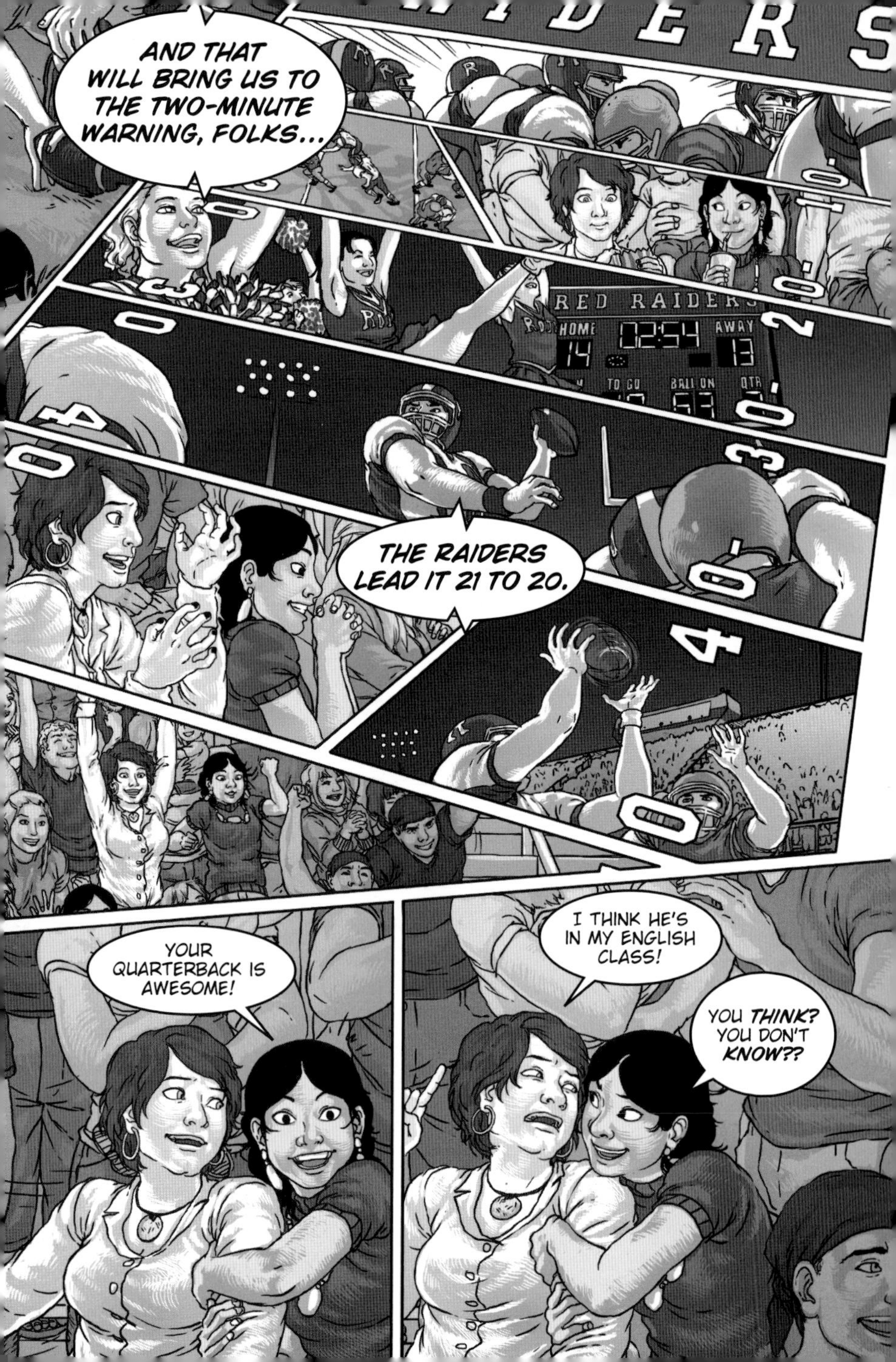
AND THAT WILL BRING US TO THE TWO-MINUTE WARNING, FOLKS...
RED RAIDERS
HOME
AWAY
14
13
TO GO
BALL ON
QTR
THE RAIDERS LEAD IT 21 TO 20.
YOUR QUARTERBACK IS AWESOME!
I THINK HE'S IN MY ENGLISH CLASS!
YOU *THINK*? YOU DON'T *KNOW*??

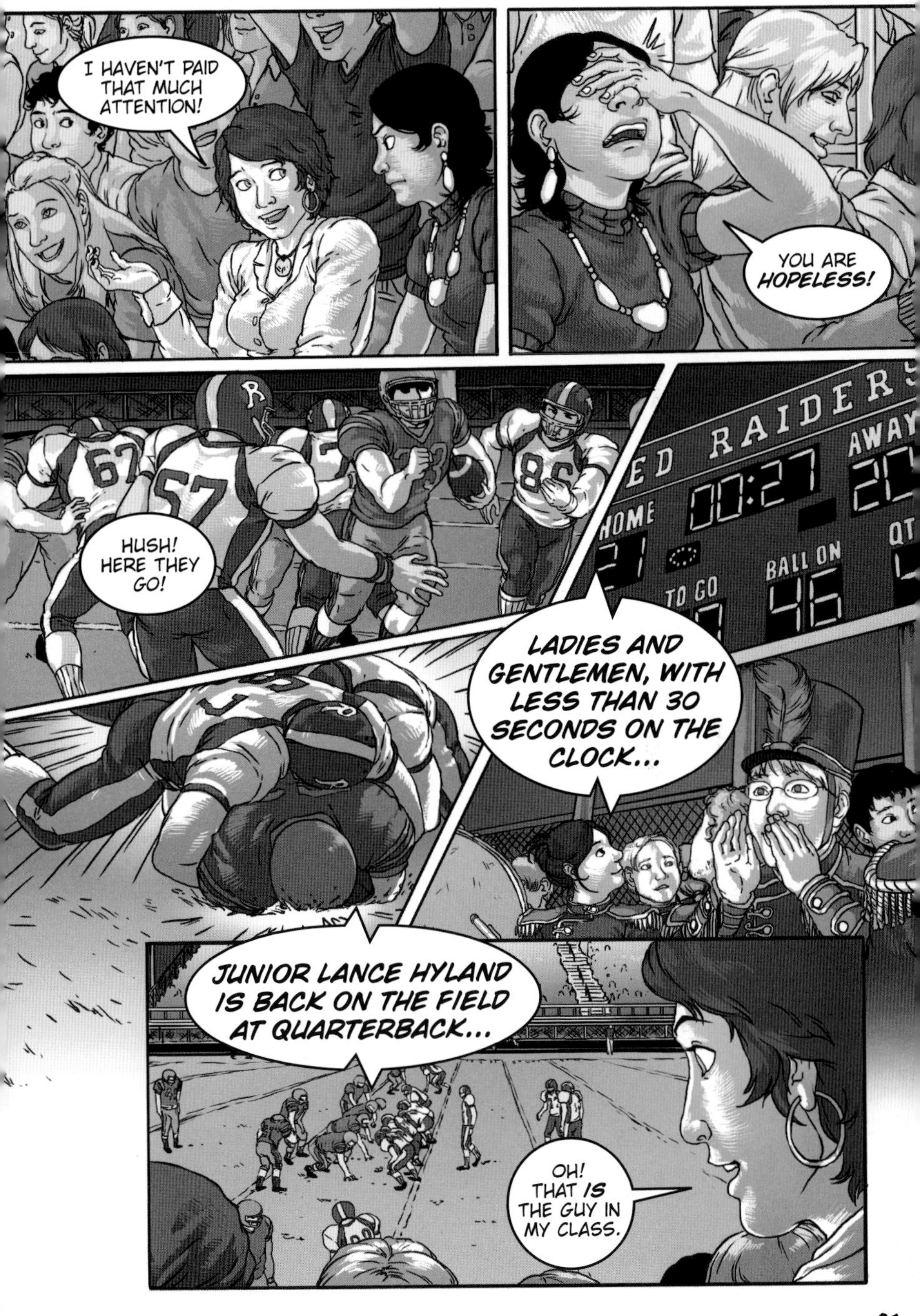
I HAVEN'T PAID THAT MUCH ATTENTION!
YOU ARE *HOPELESS!*
RED RAIDERS
HOME
AWAY
QTR
BALL ON
TO GO
00:27
46
HUSH! HERE THEY GO!
LADIES AND GENTLEMEN, WITH LESS THAN 30 SECONDS ON THE CLOCK...
JUNIOR LANCE HYLAND IS BACK ON THE FIELD AT QUARTERBACK...
OH! THAT *IS* THE GUY IN MY CLASS.

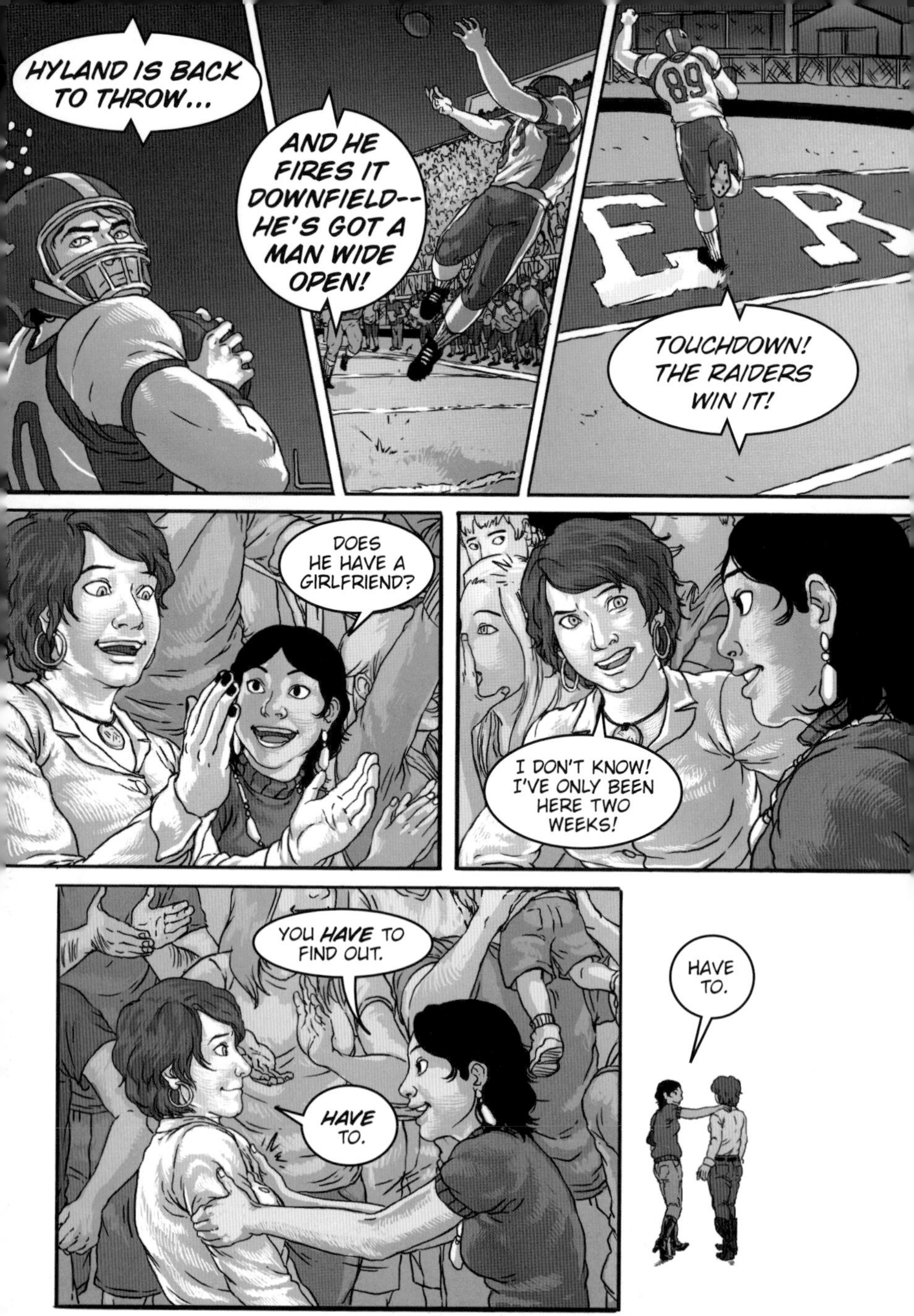
HYLAND IS BACK TO THROW...
AND HE FIRES IT DOWNFIELD--HE'S GOT A MAN WIDE OPEN!
TOUCHDOWN! THE RAIDERS WIN IT!
DOES HE HAVE A GIRLFRIEND?
I DON'T KNOW! I'VE ONLY BEEN HERE TWO WEEKS!
YOU HAVE TO FIND OUT.
HAVE TO.
HAVE TO.

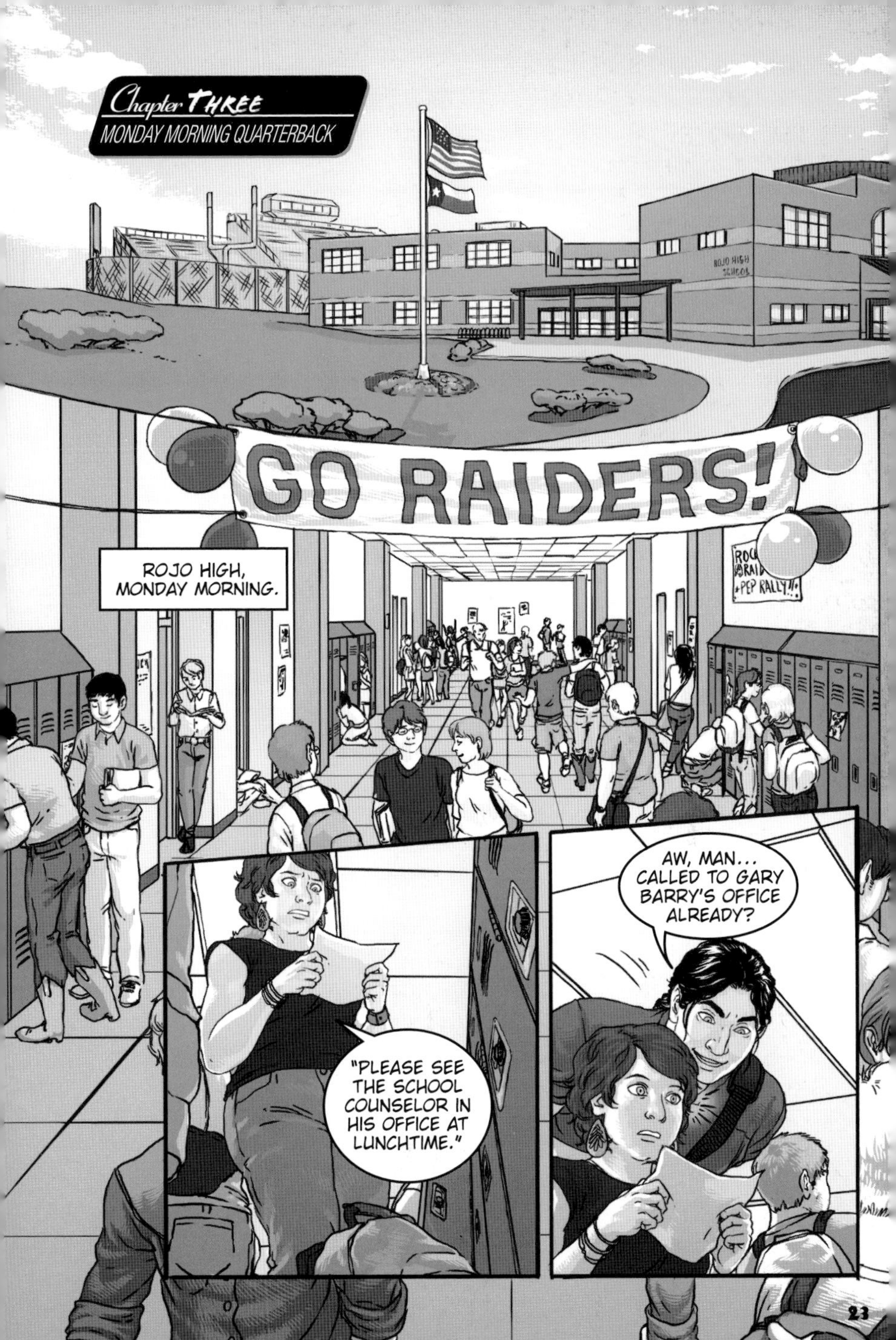
Chapter THREE
MONDAY MORNING QUARTERBACK
ROJO HIGH SCHOOL
GO RAIDERS!
ROJO HIGH, MONDAY MORNING.
"PLEASE SEE THE SCHOOL COUNSELOR IN HIS OFFICE AT LUNCHTIME."
AW, MAN... CALLED TO GARY BARRY'S OFFICE ALREADY?

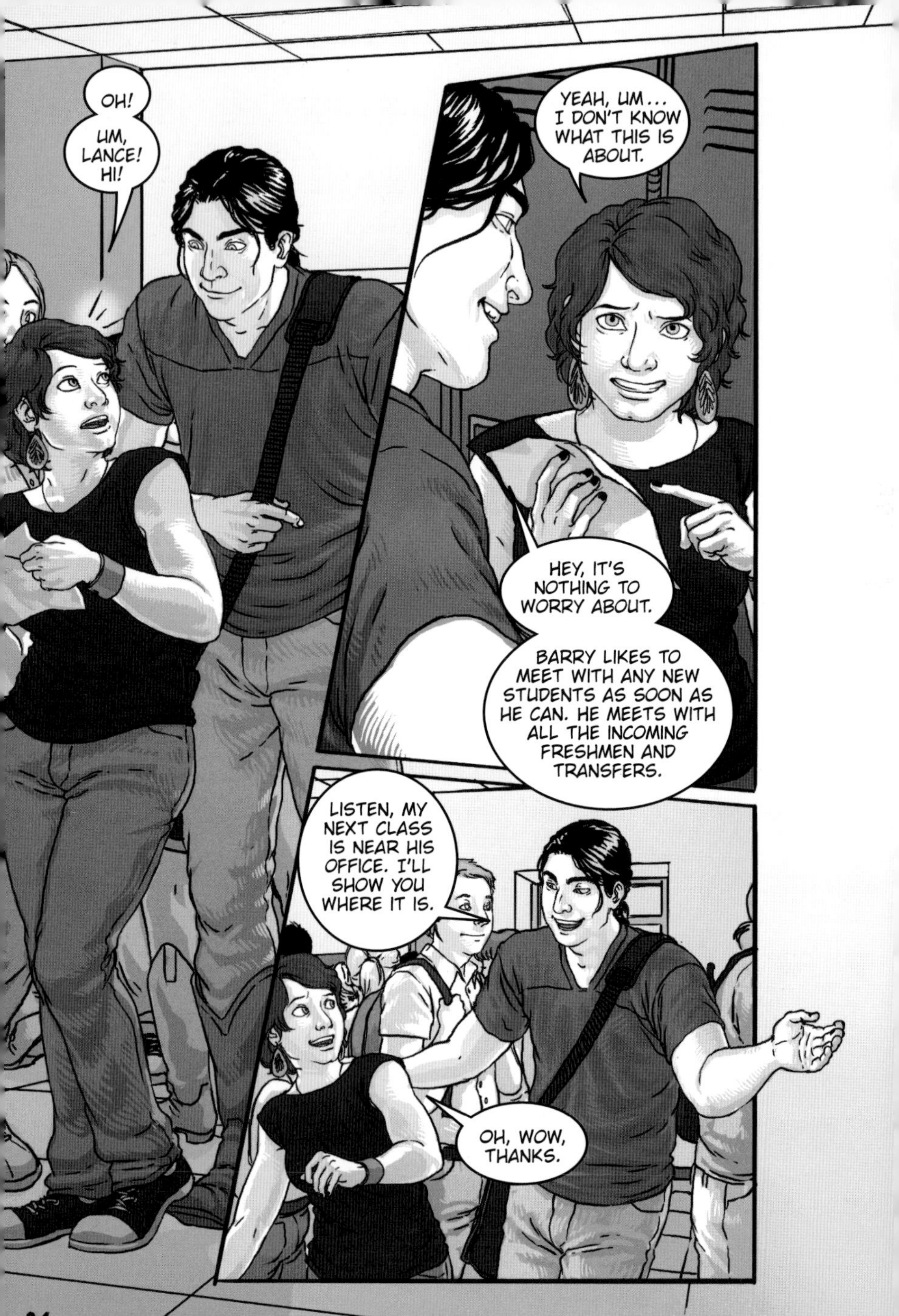
OH!
UM, LANCE! HI!
YEAH, UM... I DON'T KNOW WHAT THIS IS ABOUT.
HEY, IT'S NOTHING TO WORRY ABOUT.
BARRY LIKES TO MEET WITH ANY NEW STUDENTS AS SOON AS HE CAN. HE MEETS WITH ALL THE INCOMING FRESHMEN AND TRANSFERS.
LISTEN, MY NEXT CLASS IS NEAR HIS OFFICE. I'LL SHOW YOU WHERE IT IS.
OH, WOW, THANKS.

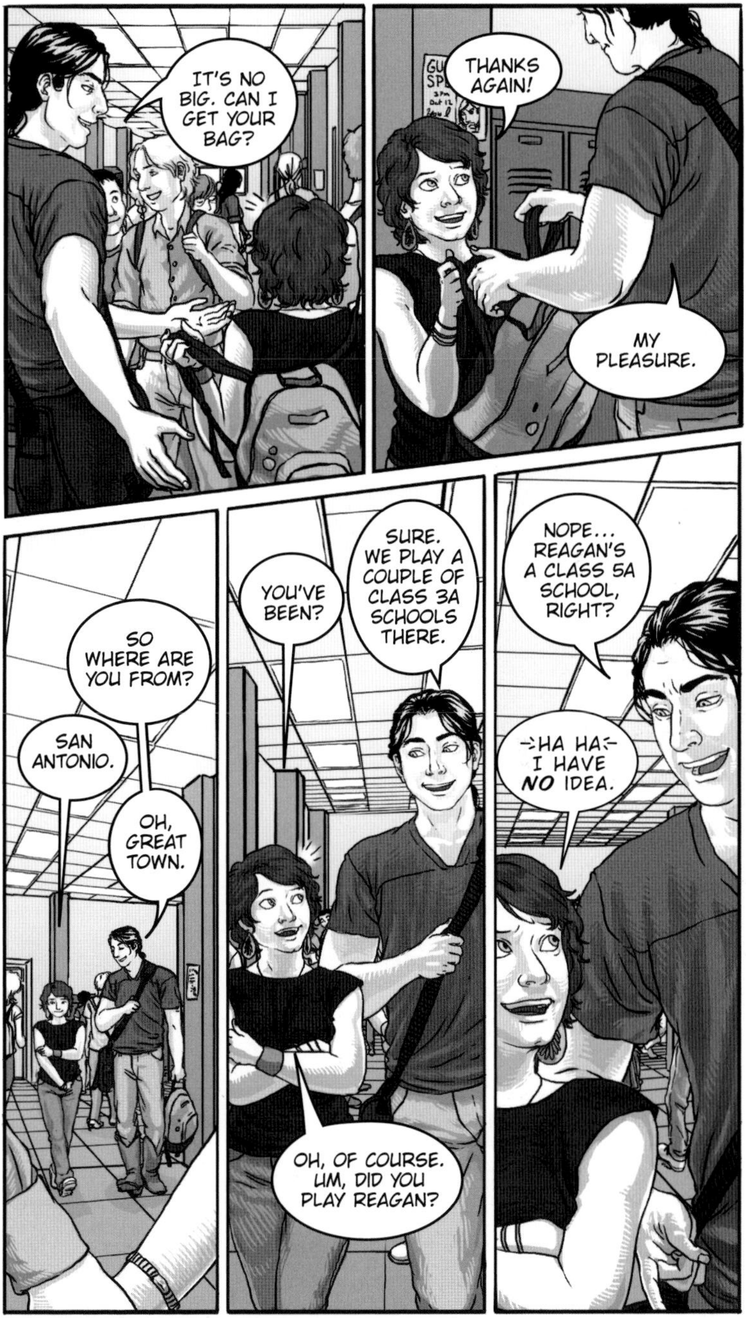
IT'S NO BIG. CAN I GET YOUR BAG?
THANKS AGAIN!
MY PLEASURE.
SO WHERE ARE YOU FROM?
SAN ANTONIO.
OH, GREAT TOWN.
YOU'VE BEEN?
SURE. WE PLAY A COUPLE OF CLASS 3A SCHOOLS THERE.
OH, OF COURSE. UM, DID YOU PLAY REAGAN?
NOPE... REAGAN'S A CLASS 5A SCHOOL, RIGHT?
HA HA I HAVE ***NO*** IDEA.

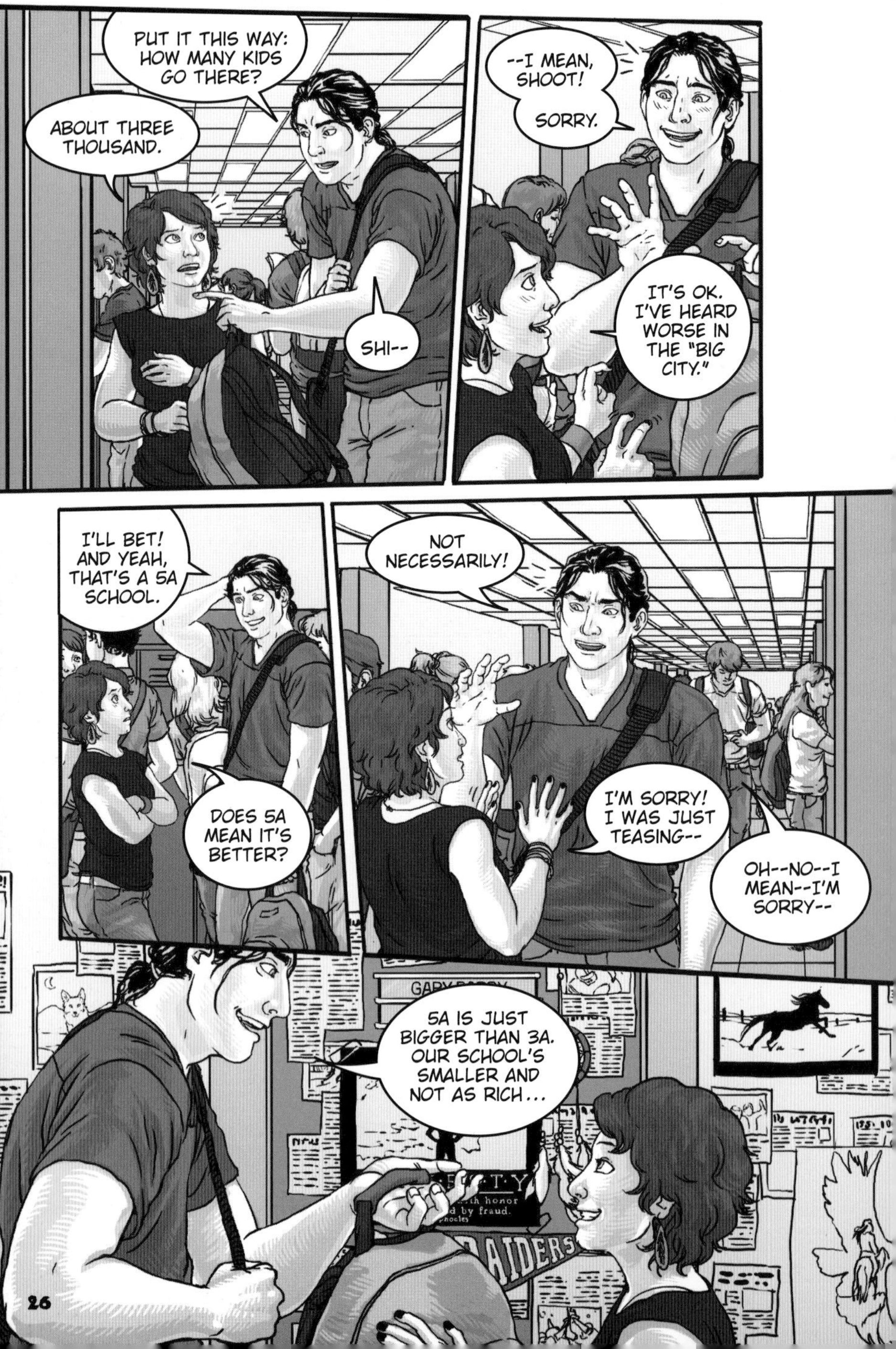
PUT IT THIS WAY: HOW MANY KIDS GO THERE?
ABOUT THREE THOUSAND.
SHI--
--I MEAN, SHOOT!
SORRY.
IT'S OK. I'VE HEARD WORSE IN THE "BIG CITY."
I'LL BET! AND YEAH, THAT'S A 5A SCHOOL.
DOES 5A MEAN IT'S BETTER?
NOT NECESSARILY!
I'M SORRY! I WAS JUST TEASING--
OH--NO--I MEAN--I'M SORRY--
5A IS JUST BIGGER THAN 3A. OUR SCHOOL'S SMALLER AND NOT AS RICH...

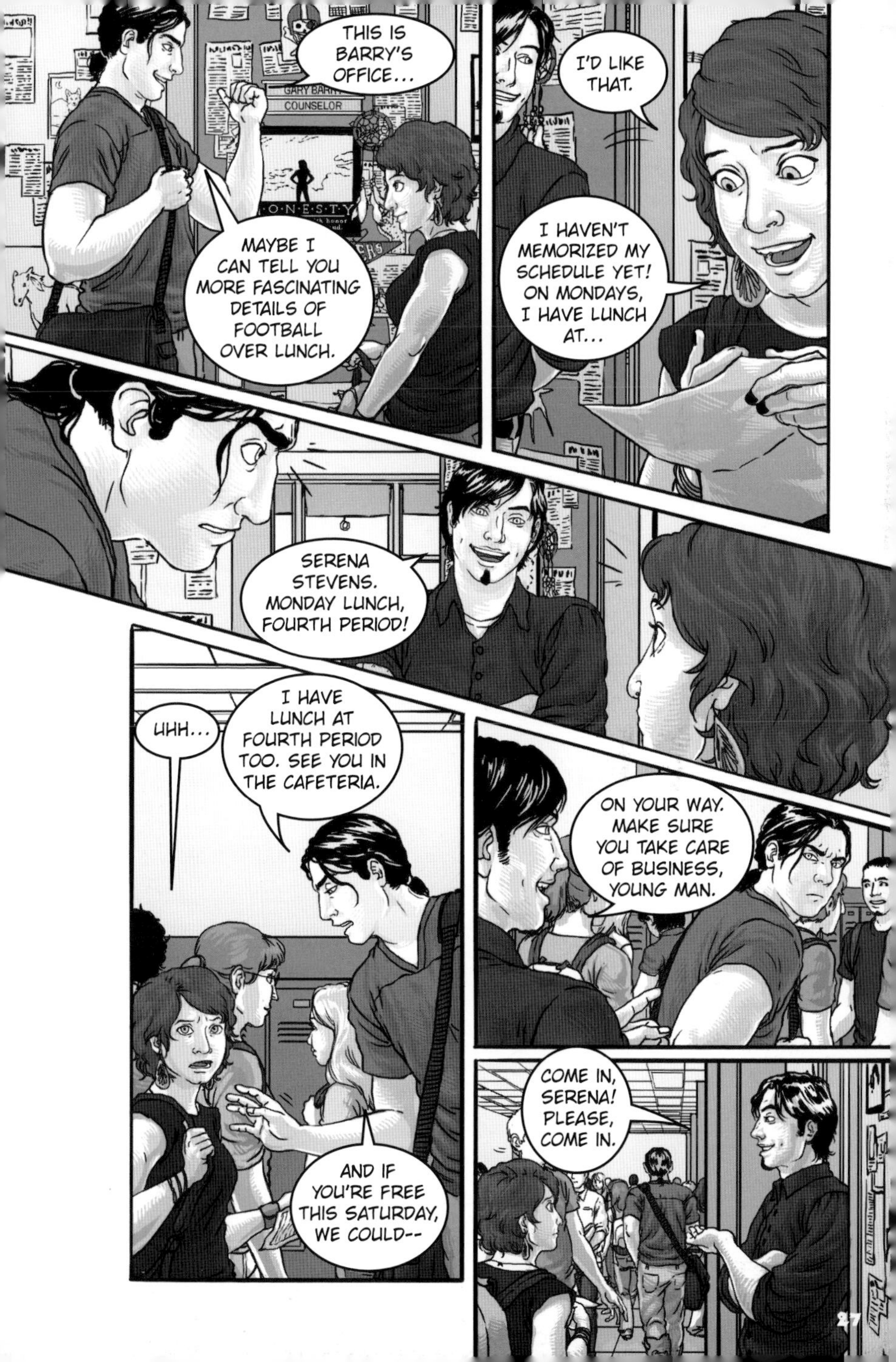
THIS IS BARRY'S OFFICE...
COUNSELOR
MAYBE I CAN TELL YOU MORE FASCINATING DETAILS OF FOOTBALL OVER LUNCH.
I'D LIKE THAT.
I HAVEN'T MEMORIZED MY SCHEDULE YET! ON MONDAYS, I HAVE LUNCH AT...
SERENA STEVENS. MONDAY LUNCH, FOURTH PERIOD!
UHH...
I HAVE LUNCH AT FOURTH PERIOD TOO. SEE YOU IN THE CAFETERIA.
AND IF YOU'RE FREE THIS SATURDAY, WE COULD--
ON YOUR WAY. MAKE SURE YOU TAKE CARE OF BUSINESS, YOUNG MAN.
COME IN, SERENA! PLEASE, COME IN.

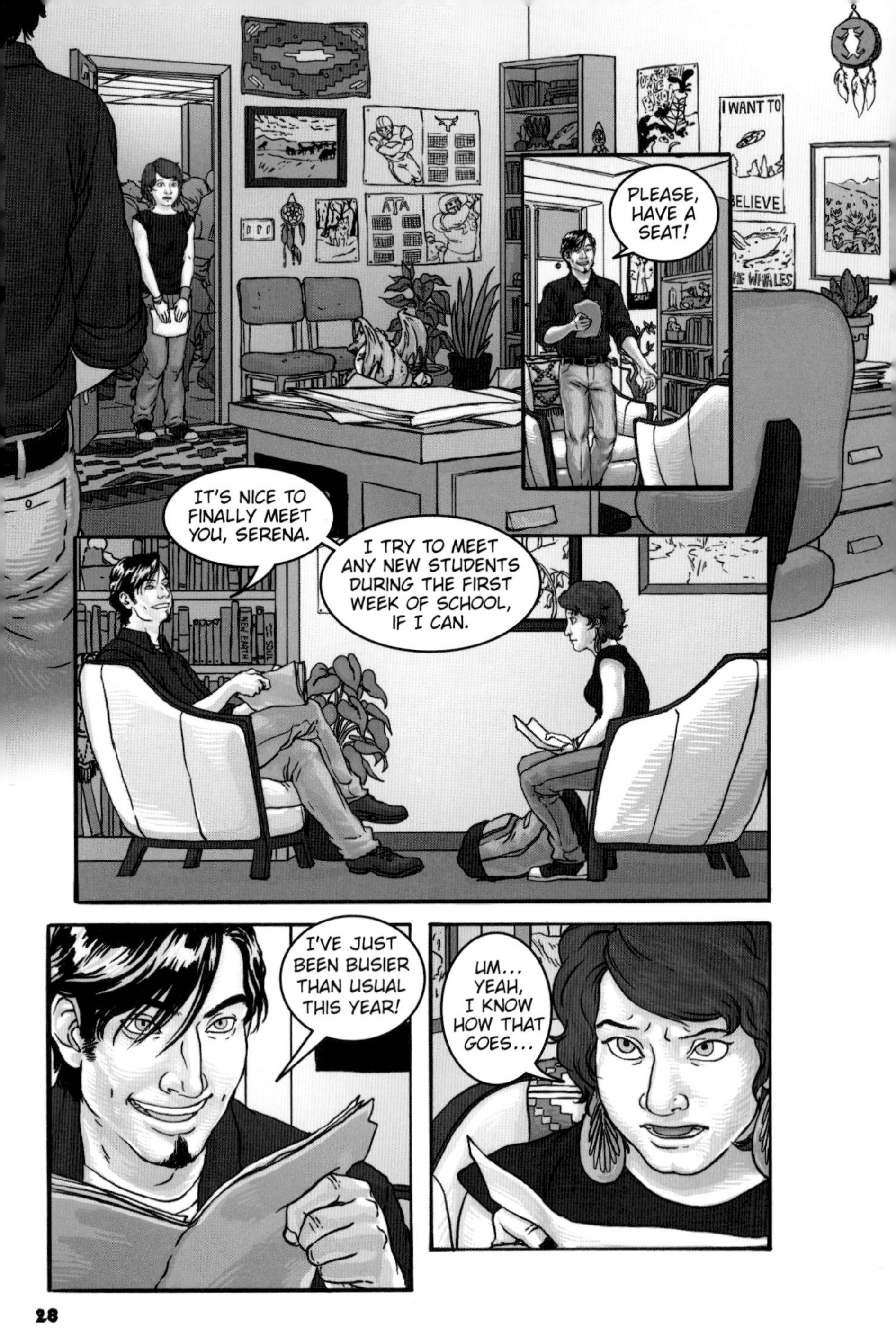
I WANT TO
BELIEVE
THE WHALES
PLEASE, HAVE A SEAT!
IT'S NICE TO FINALLY MEET YOU, SERENA.
I TRY TO MEET ANY NEW STUDENTS DURING THE FIRST WEEK OF SCHOOL, IF I CAN.
NEW EARTH
SOUL
I'VE JUST BEEN BUSIER THAN USUAL THIS YEAR!
UM... YEAH, I KNOW HOW THAT GOES...

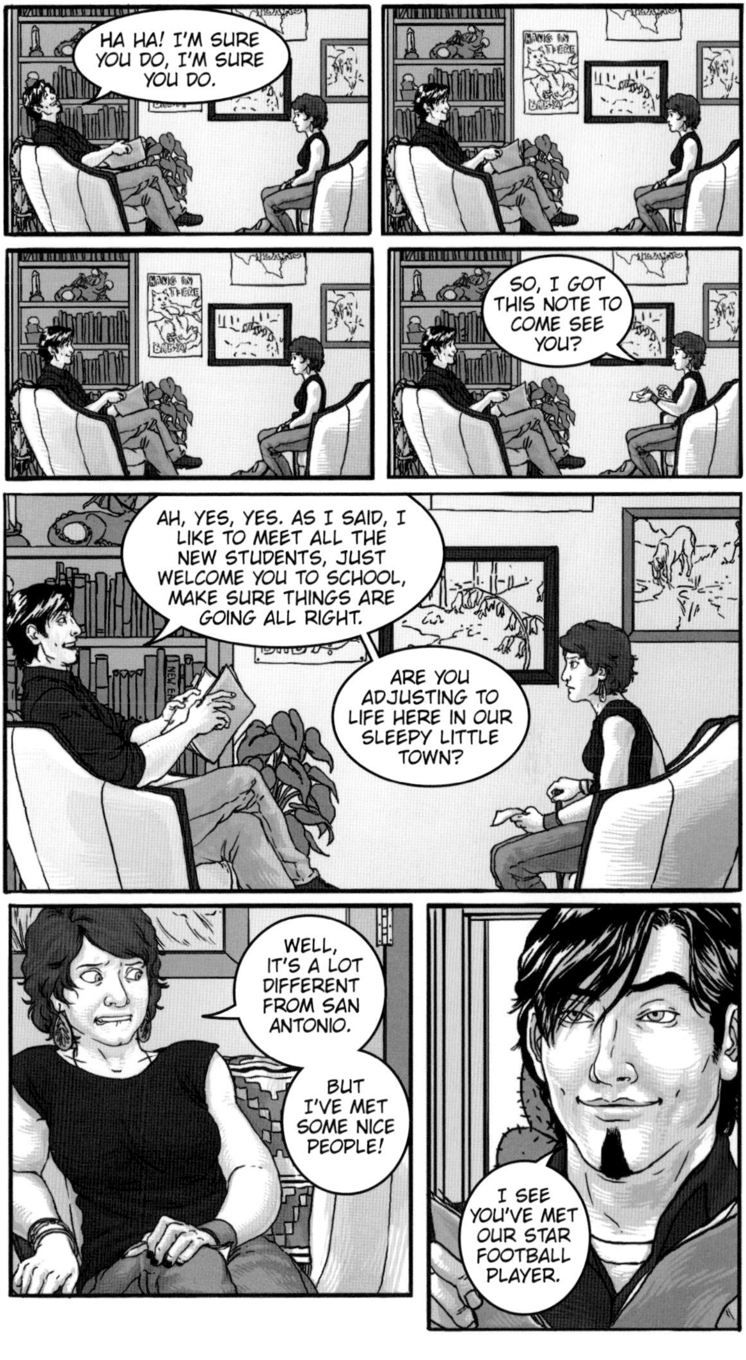
HA HA! I'M SURE YOU DO, I'M SURE YOU DO.
HANG IN THERE BABY!
SO, I GOT THIS NOTE TO COME SEE YOU?
AH, YES, YES. AS I SAID, I LIKE TO MEET ALL THE NEW STUDENTS, JUST WELCOME YOU TO SCHOOL, MAKE SURE THINGS ARE GOING ALL RIGHT.
ARE YOU ADJUSTING TO LIFE HERE IN OUR SLEEPY LITTLE TOWN?
WELL, IT'S A LOT DIFFERENT FROM SAN ANTONIO.
BUT I'VE MET SOME NICE PEOPLE!
I SEE YOU'VE MET OUR STAR FOOTBALL PLAYER.

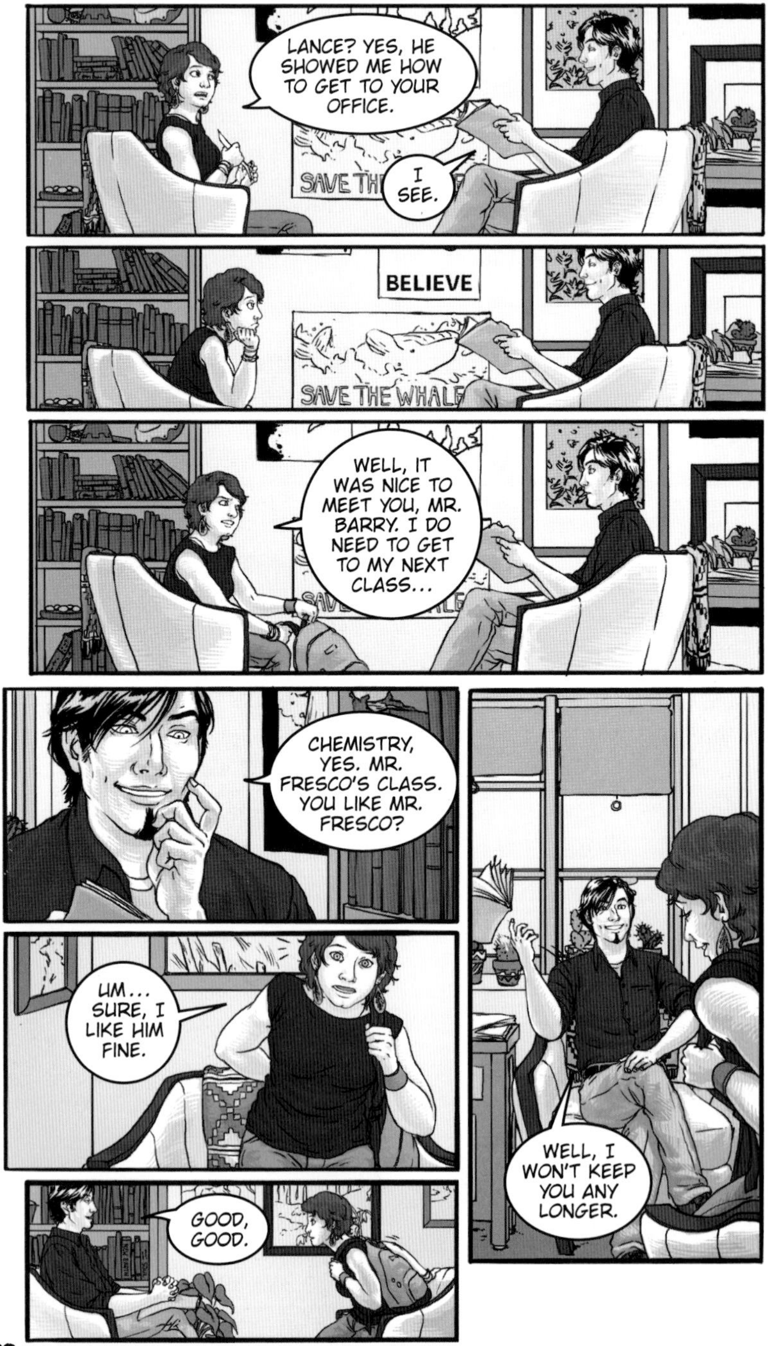
LANCE? YES, HE SHOWED ME HOW TO GET TO YOUR OFFICE.
I SEE.
SAVE THE
BELIEVE
SAVE THE WHALE
WELL, IT WAS NICE TO MEET YOU, MR. BARRY. I DO NEED TO GET TO MY NEXT CLASS...
CHEMISTRY, YES. MR. FRESCO'S CLASS. YOU LIKE MR. FRESCO?
UM... SURE, I LIKE HIM FINE.
GOOD, GOOD.
WELL, I WON'T KEEP YOU ANY LONGER.

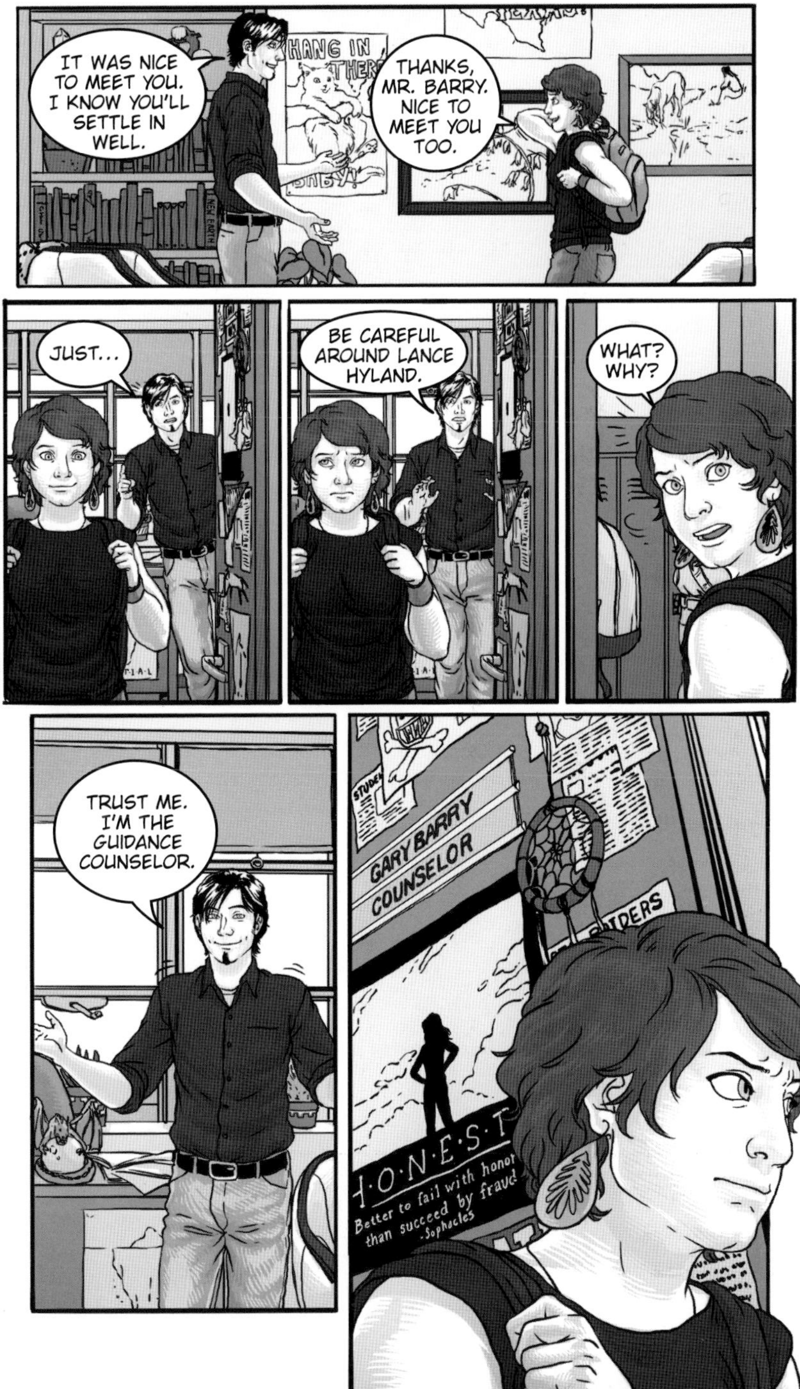
IT WAS NICE TO MEET YOU. I KNOW YOU'LL SETTLE IN WELL.
HANG IN THERE BABY!
THANKS, MR. BARRY. NICE TO MEET YOU TOO.
JUST...
BE CAREFUL AROUND LANCE HYLAND.
WHAT? WHY?
TRUST ME. I'M THE GUIDANCE COUNSELOR.
GARY BARRY
COUNSELOR
RAIDERS
H·O·N·E·S·T
Better to fail with honor than succeed by fraud.
-Sophocles

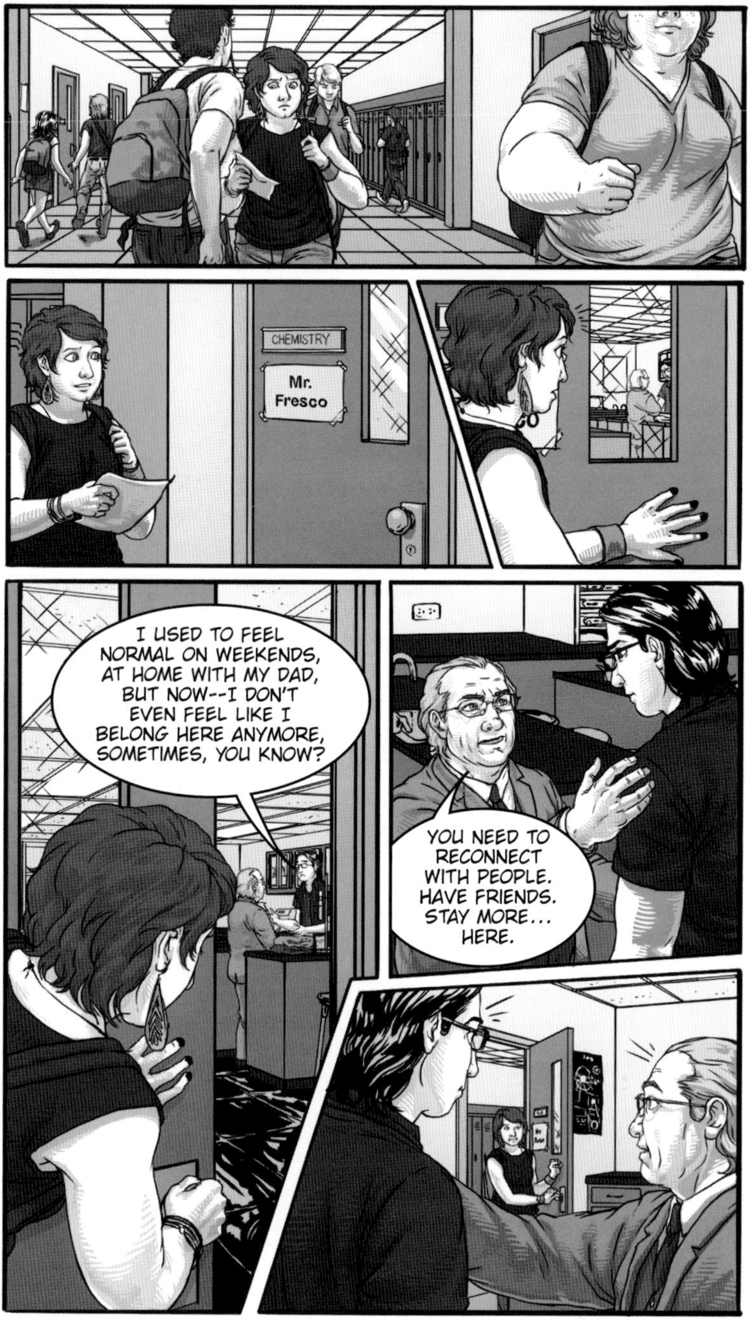
CHEMISTRY
Mr. Fresco
I USED TO FEEL NORMAL ON WEEKENDS, AT HOME WITH MY DAD, BUT NOW--I DON'T EVEN FEEL LIKE I BELONG HERE ANYMORE, SOMETIMES, YOU KNOW?
YOU NEED TO RECONNECT WITH PEOPLE. HAVE FRIENDS. STAY MORE... HERE.

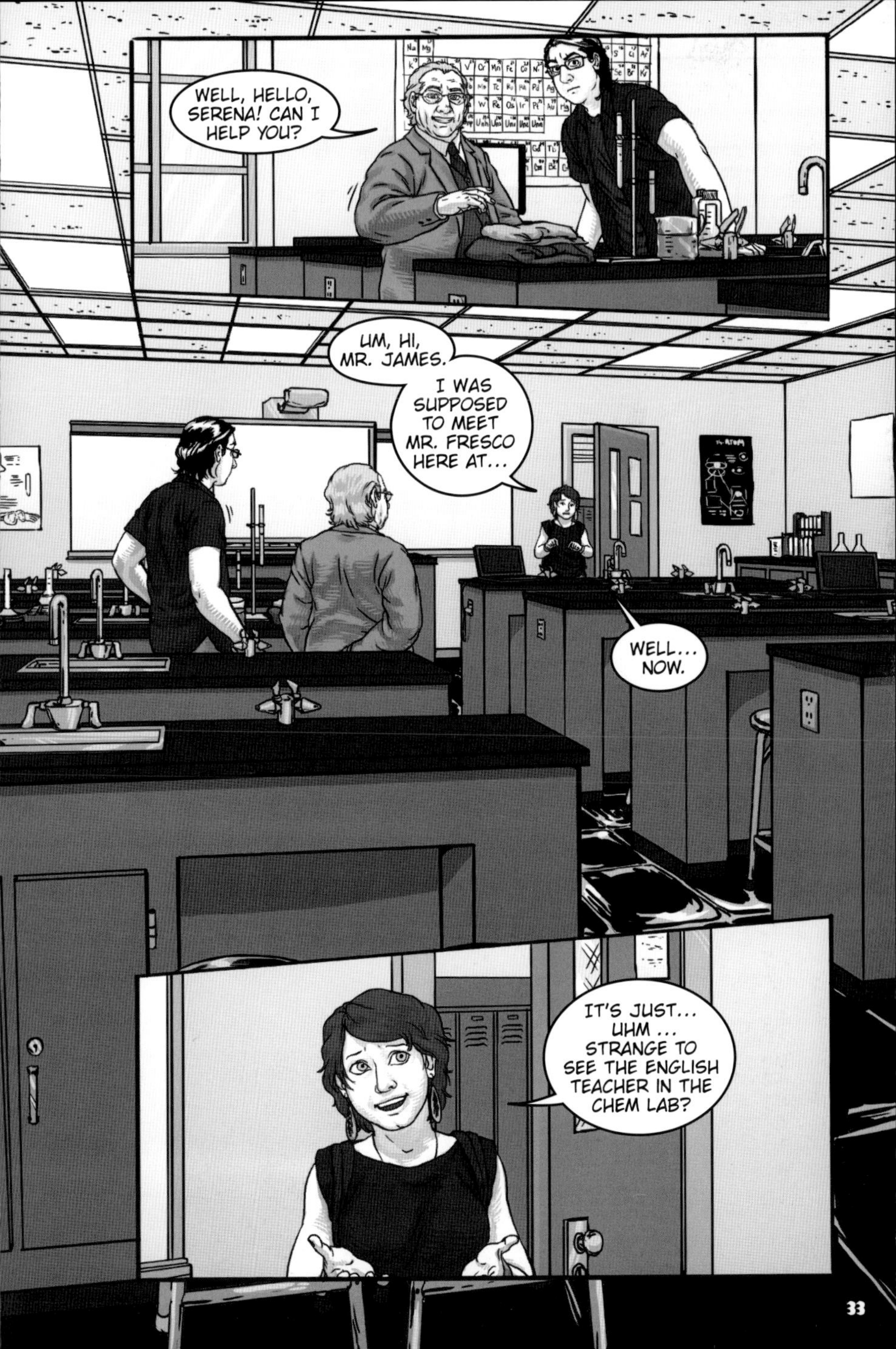
WELL, HELLO, SERENA! CAN I HELP YOU?
UM, HI, MR. JAMES.
I WAS SUPPOSED TO MEET MR. FRESCO HERE AT...
WELL... NOW.
IT'S JUST... UHM ... STRANGE TO SEE THE ENGLISH TEACHER IN THE CHEM LAB?

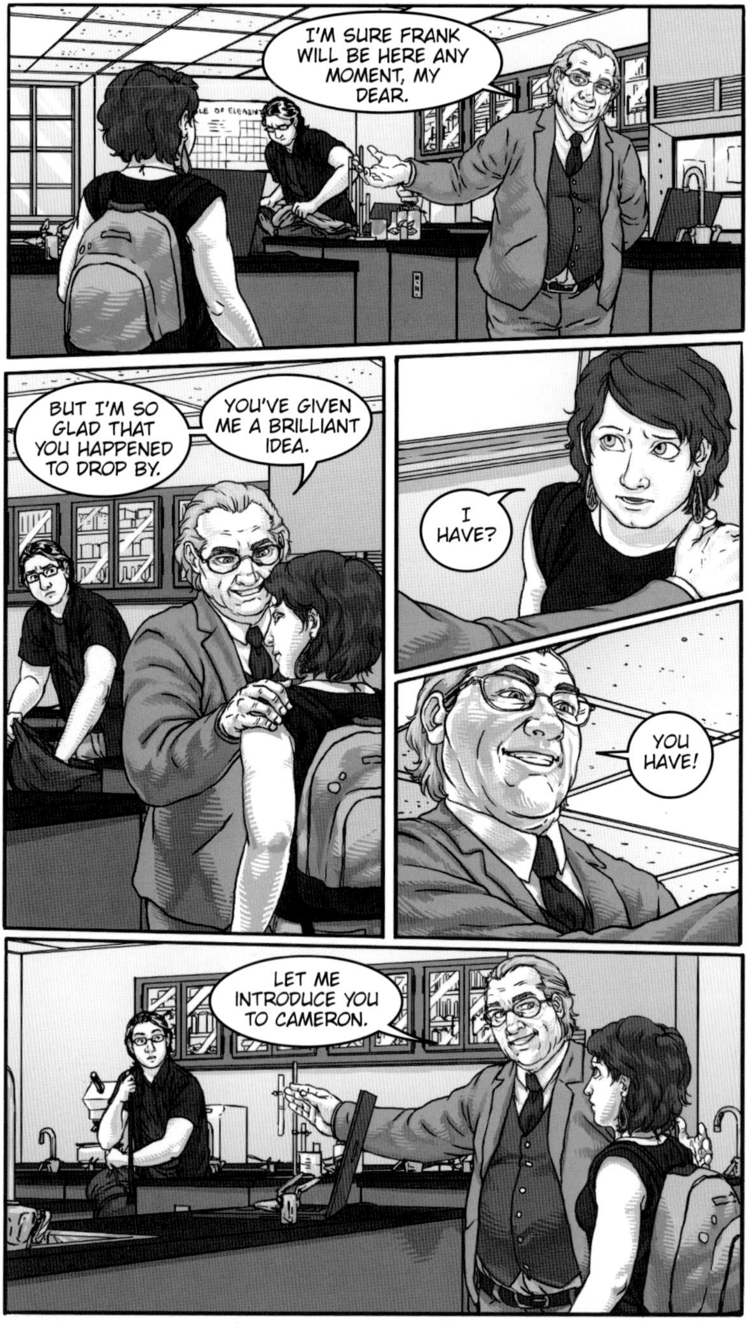
I'M SURE FRANK WILL BE HERE ANY MOMENT, MY DEAR.
BUT I'M SO GLAD THAT YOU HAPPENED TO DROP BY.
YOU'VE GIVEN ME A BRILLIANT IDEA.
I HAVE?
YOU HAVE!
LET ME INTRODUCE YOU TO CAMERON.

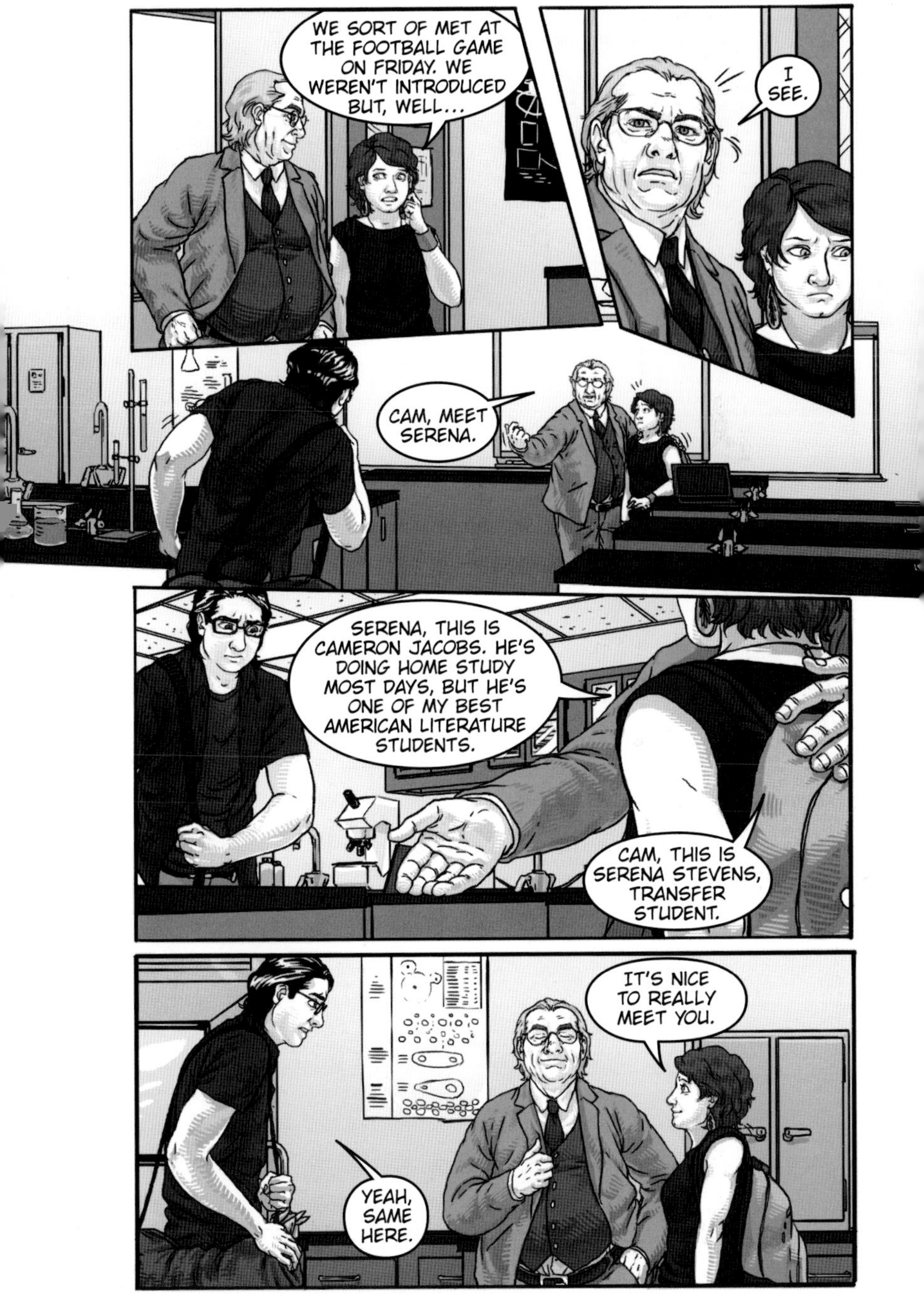
WE SORT OF MET AT THE FOOTBALL GAME ON FRIDAY. WE WEREN'T INTRODUCED BUT, WELL...
I SEE.
CAM, MEET SERENA.
SERENA, THIS IS CAMERON JACOBS. HE'S DOING HOME STUDY MOST DAYS, BUT HE'S ONE OF MY BEST AMERICAN LITERATURE STUDENTS.
CAM, THIS IS SERENA STEVENS, TRANSFER STUDENT.
IT'S NICE TO REALLY MEET YOU.
YEAH, SAME HERE.

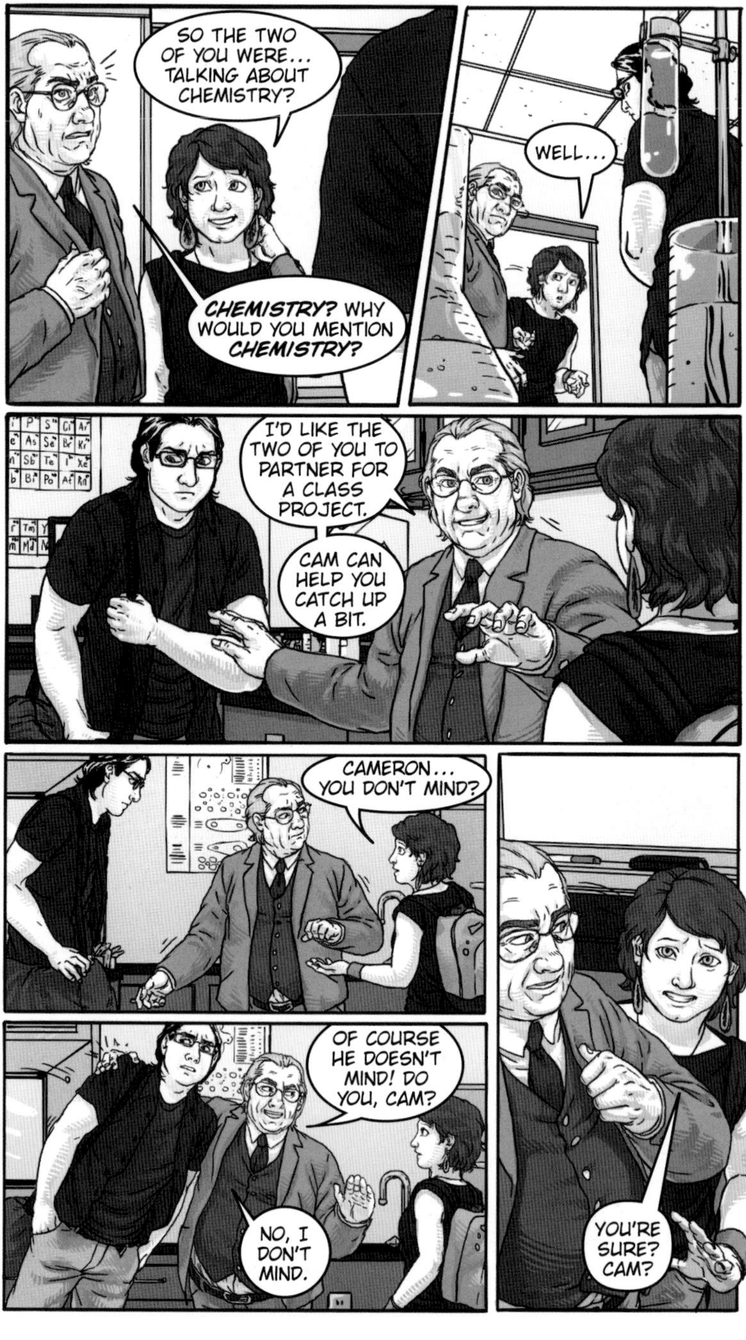
SO THE TWO OF YOU WERE... TALKING ABOUT CHEMISTRY?
CHEMISTRY? WHY WOULD YOU MENTION *CHEMISTRY?*
WELL...
I'D LIKE THE TWO OF YOU TO PARTNER FOR A CLASS PROJECT.
CAM CAN HELP YOU CATCH UP A BIT.
CAMERON... YOU DON'T MIND?
OF COURSE HE DOESN'T MIND! DO YOU, CAM?
NO, I DON'T MIND.
YOU'RE SURE? CAM?

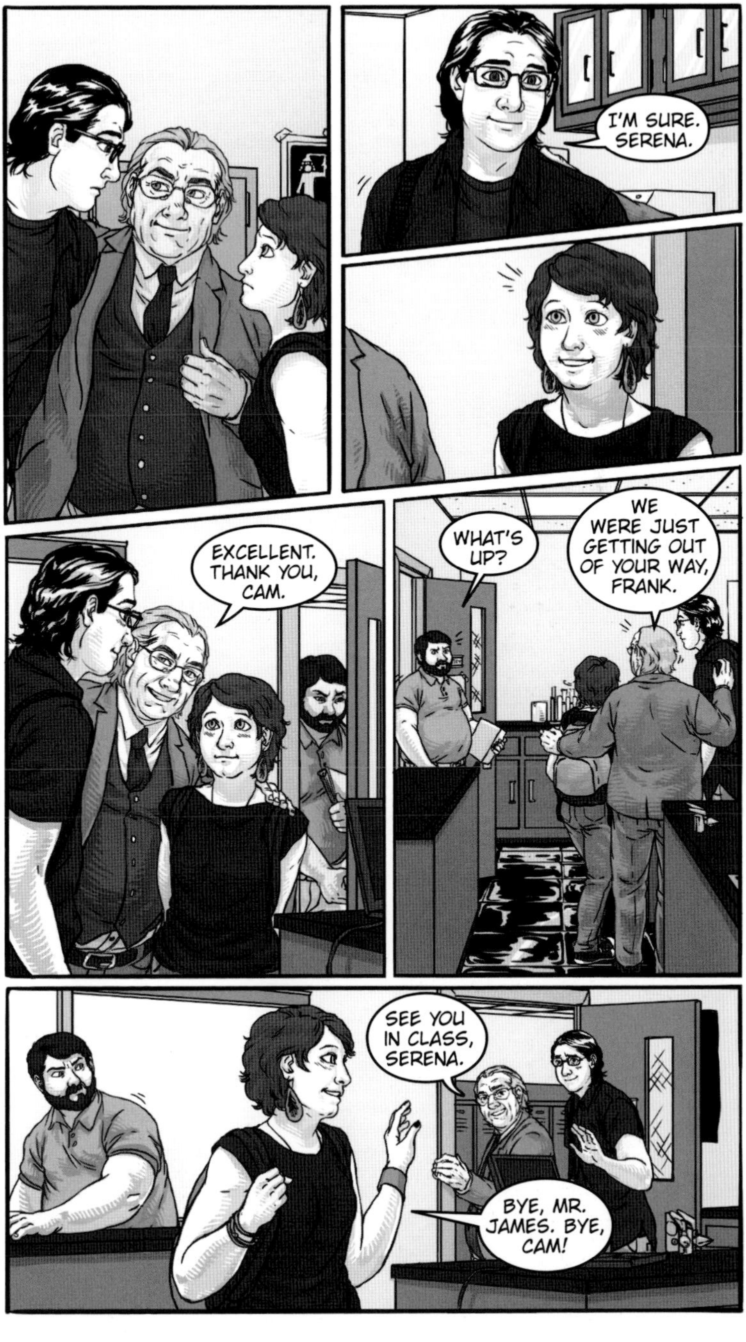
I'M SURE. SERENA.
EXCELLENT. THANK YOU, CAM.
WHAT'S UP?
WE WERE JUST GETTING OUT OF YOUR WAY, FRANK.
SEE YOU IN CLASS, SERENA.
BYE, MR. JAMES. BYE, CAM!

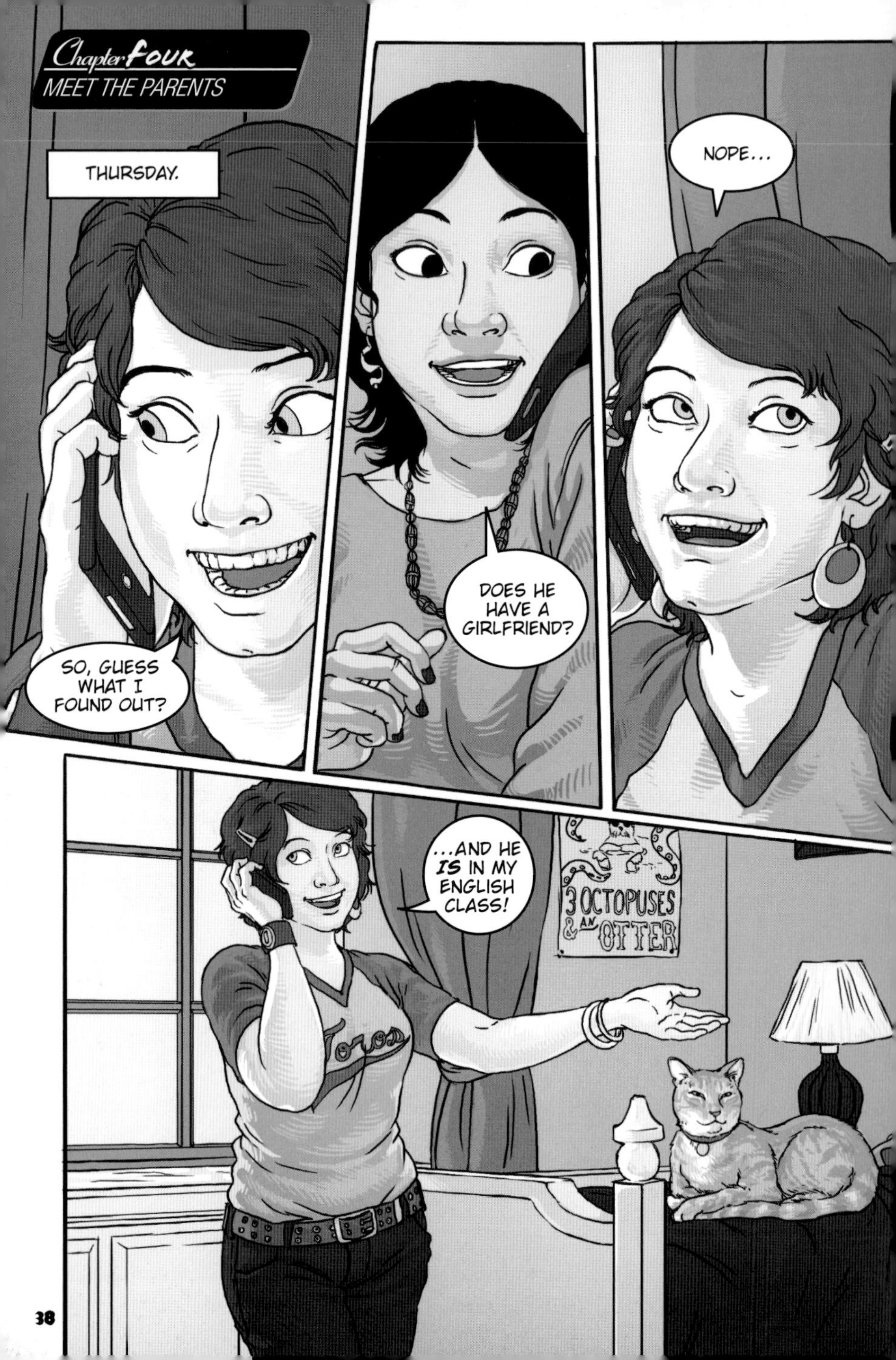
Chapter FOUR
MEET THE PARENTS
THURSDAY.
SO, GUESS WHAT I FOUND OUT?
DOES HE HAVE A GIRLFRIEND?
NOPE...
...AND HE IS IN MY ENGLISH CLASS!
3 OCTOPUSES & AN OTTER
Toros

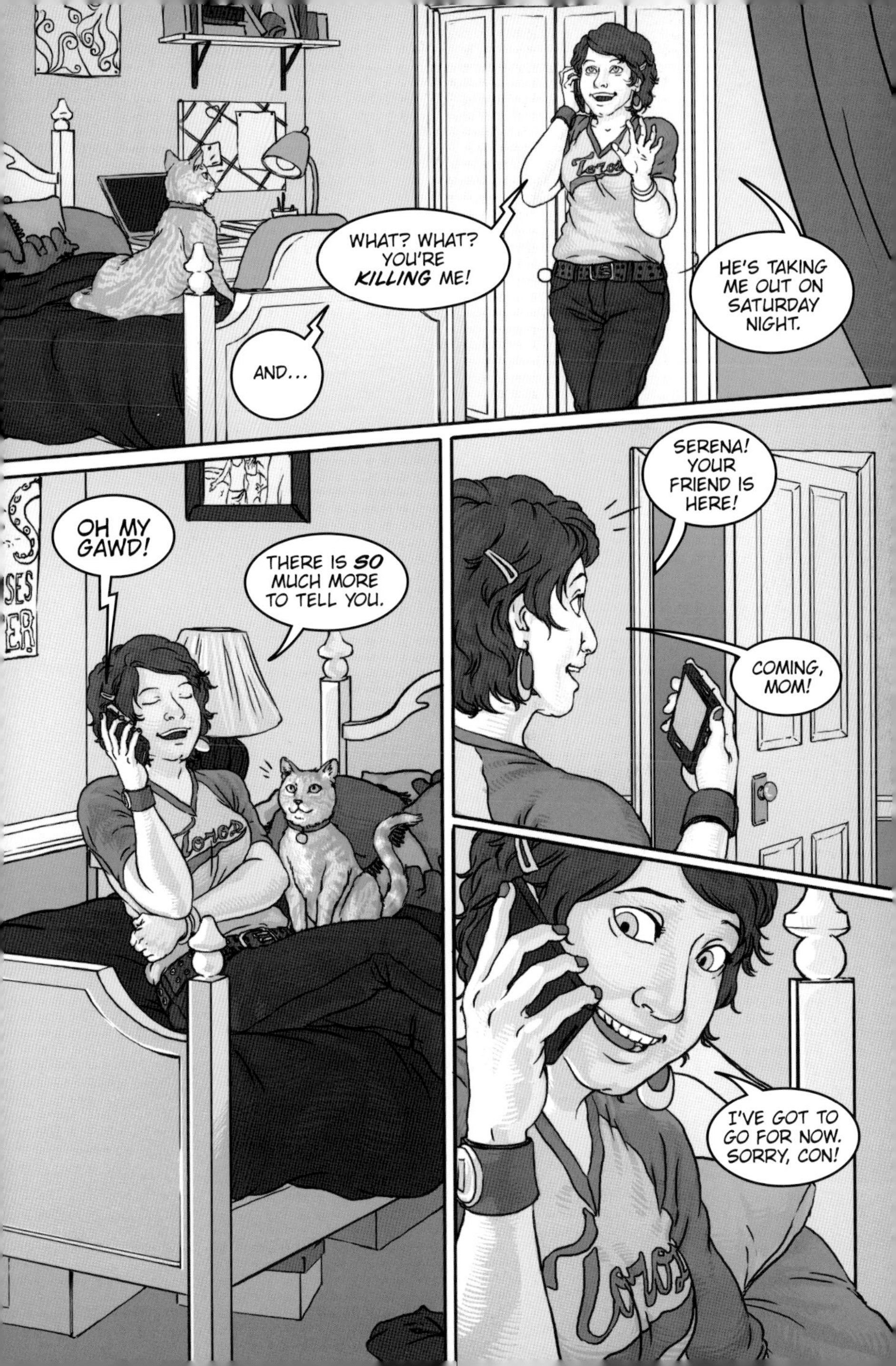
WHAT? WHAT? YOU'RE *KILLING* ME!
HE'S TAKING ME OUT ON SATURDAY NIGHT.
AND...
OH MY GAWD!
THERE IS *SO* MUCH MORE TO TELL YOU.
SERENA! YOUR FRIEND IS HERE!
COMING, MOM!
I'VE GOT TO GO FOR NOW. SORRY, CON!

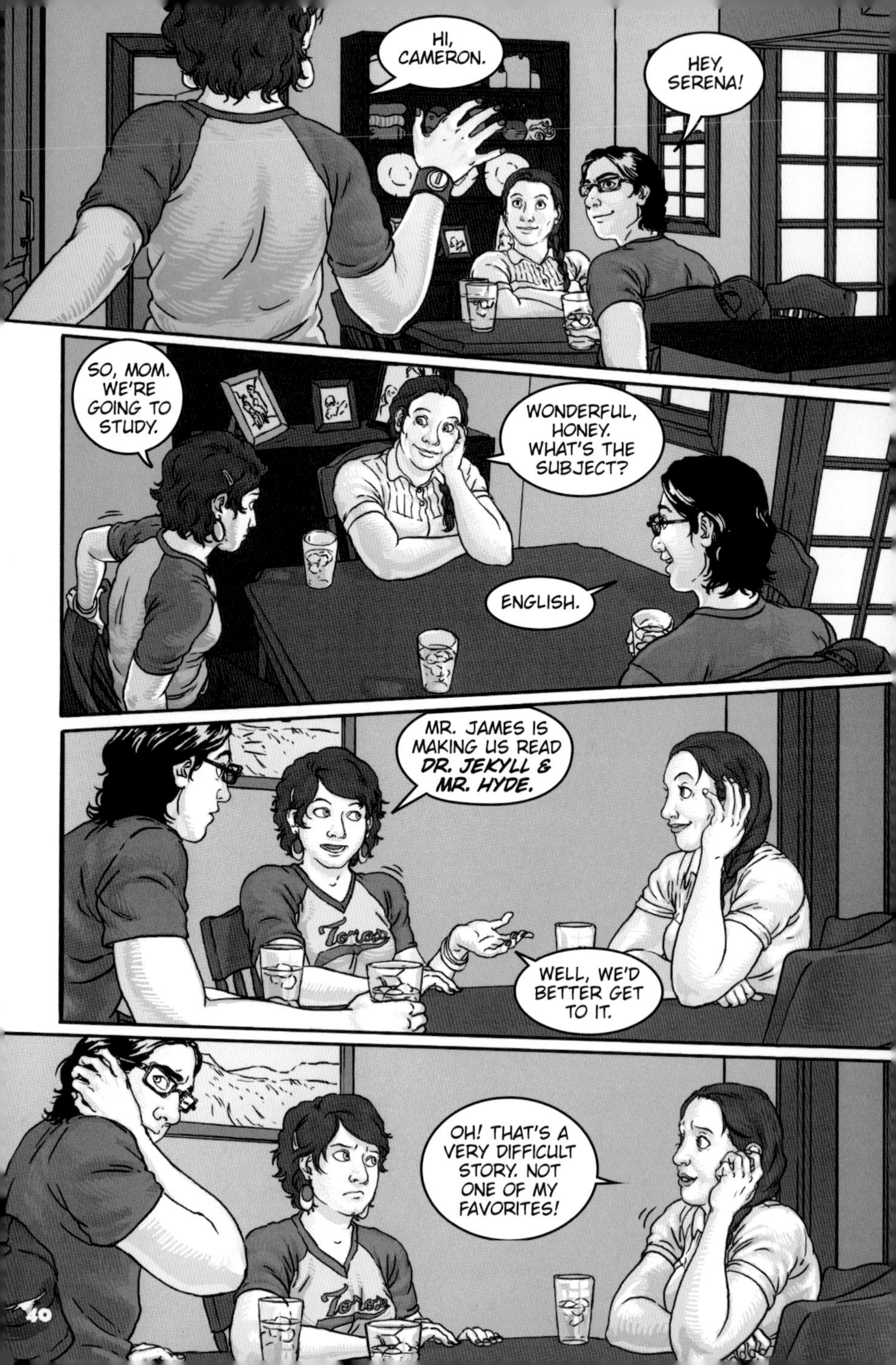
HI, CAMERON.
HEY, SERENA!
SO, MOM. WE'RE GOING TO STUDY.
WONDERFUL, HONEY. WHAT'S THE SUBJECT?
ENGLISH.
MR. JAMES IS MAKING US READ ***DR. JEKYLL & MR. HYDE.***
WELL, WE'D BETTER GET TO IT.
OH! THAT'S A VERY DIFFICULT STORY. NOT ONE OF MY FAVORITES!

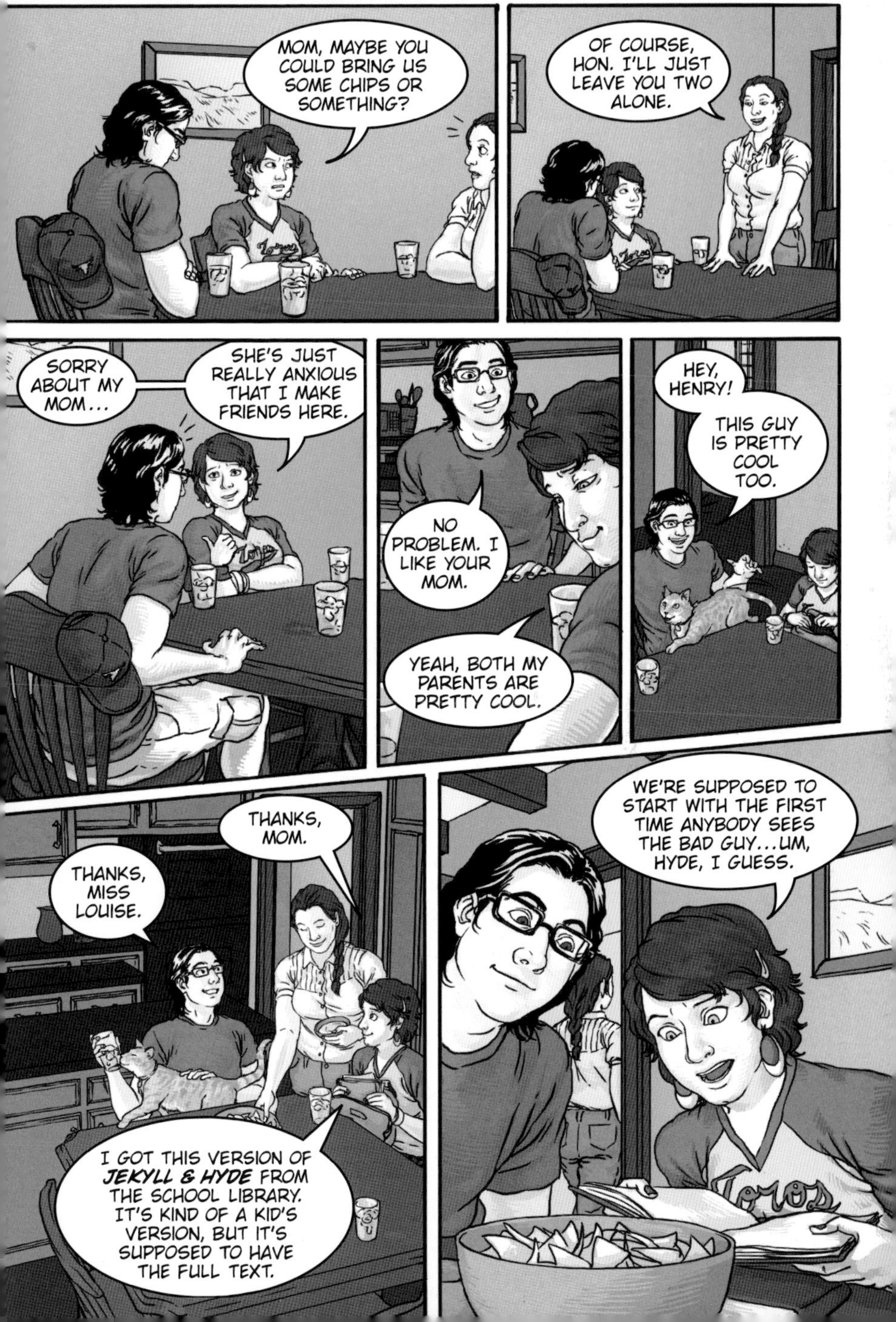
MOM, MAYBE YOU COULD BRING US SOME CHIPS OR SOMETHING?
OF COURSE, HON. I'LL JUST LEAVE YOU TWO ALONE.
SORRY ABOUT MY MOM...
SHE'S JUST REALLY ANXIOUS THAT I MAKE FRIENDS HERE.
NO PROBLEM. I LIKE YOUR MOM.
YEAH, BOTH MY PARENTS ARE PRETTY COOL.
HEY, HENRY!
THIS GUY IS PRETTY COOL TOO.
THANKS, MISS LOUISE.
THANKS, MOM.
I GOT THIS VERSION OF ***JEKYLL & HYDE*** FROM THE SCHOOL LIBRARY. IT'S KIND OF A KID'S VERSION, BUT IT'S SUPPOSED TO HAVE THE FULL TEXT.
WE'RE SUPPOSED TO START WITH THE FIRST TIME ANYBODY SEES THE BAD GUY...UM, HYDE, I GUESS.

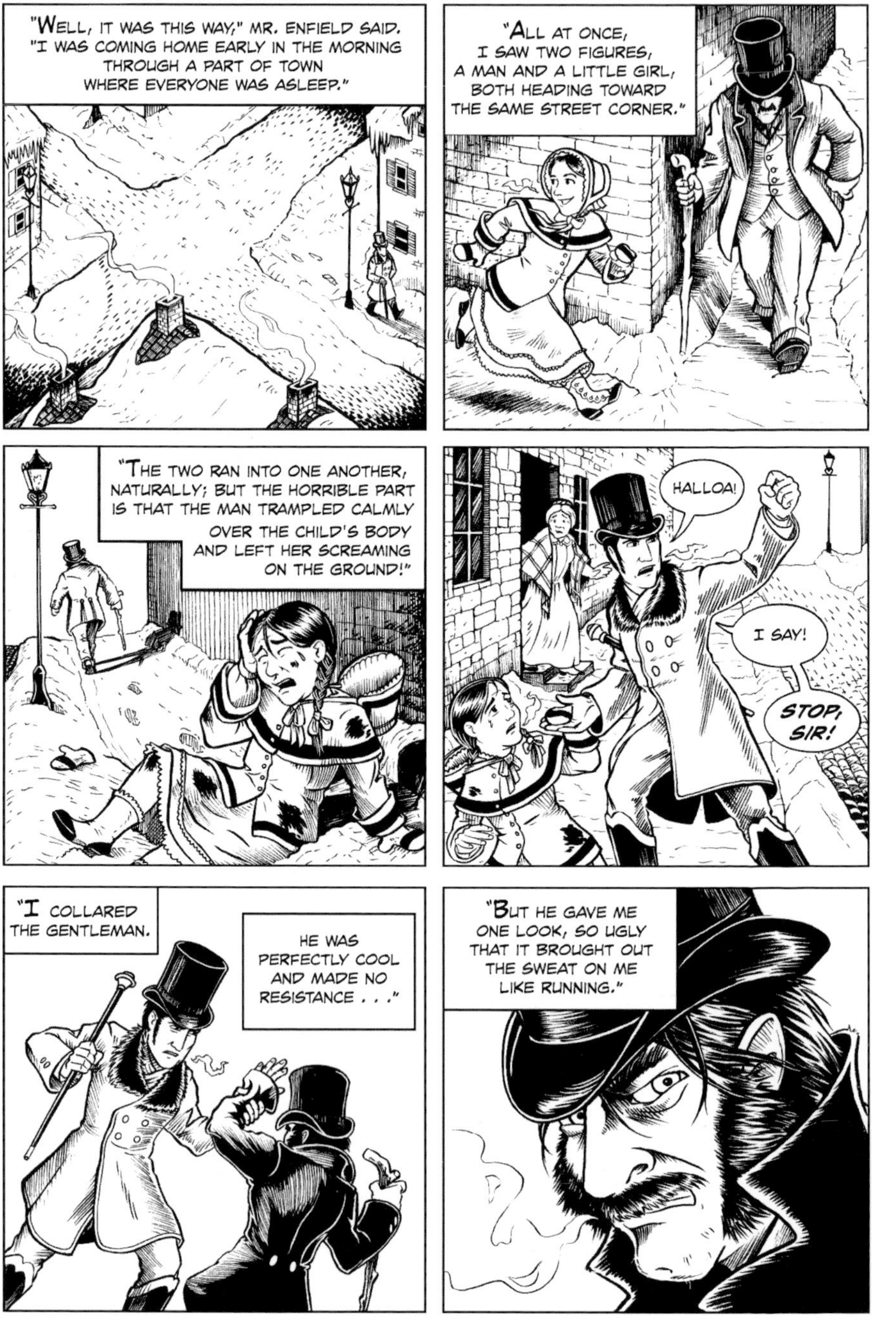
"WELL, IT WAS THIS WAY," MR. ENFIELD SAID. "I WAS COMING HOME EARLY IN THE MORNING THROUGH A PART OF TOWN WHERE EVERYONE WAS ASLEEP."
"ALL AT ONCE, I SAW TWO FIGURES, A MAN AND A LITTLE GIRL, BOTH HEADING TOWARD THE SAME STREET CORNER."
"THE TWO RAN INTO ONE ANOTHER, NATURALLY; BUT THE HORRIBLE PART IS THAT THE MAN TRAMPLED CALMLY OVER THE CHILD'S BODY AND LEFT HER SCREAMING ON THE GROUND!"
HALLOA!
I SAY!
STOP, SIR!
"I COLLARED THE GENTLEMAN.
HE WAS PERFECTLY COOL AND MADE NO RESISTANCE . . ."
"BUT HE GAVE ME ONE LOOK, SO UGLY THAT IT BROUGHT OUT THE SWEAT ON ME LIKE RUNNING."

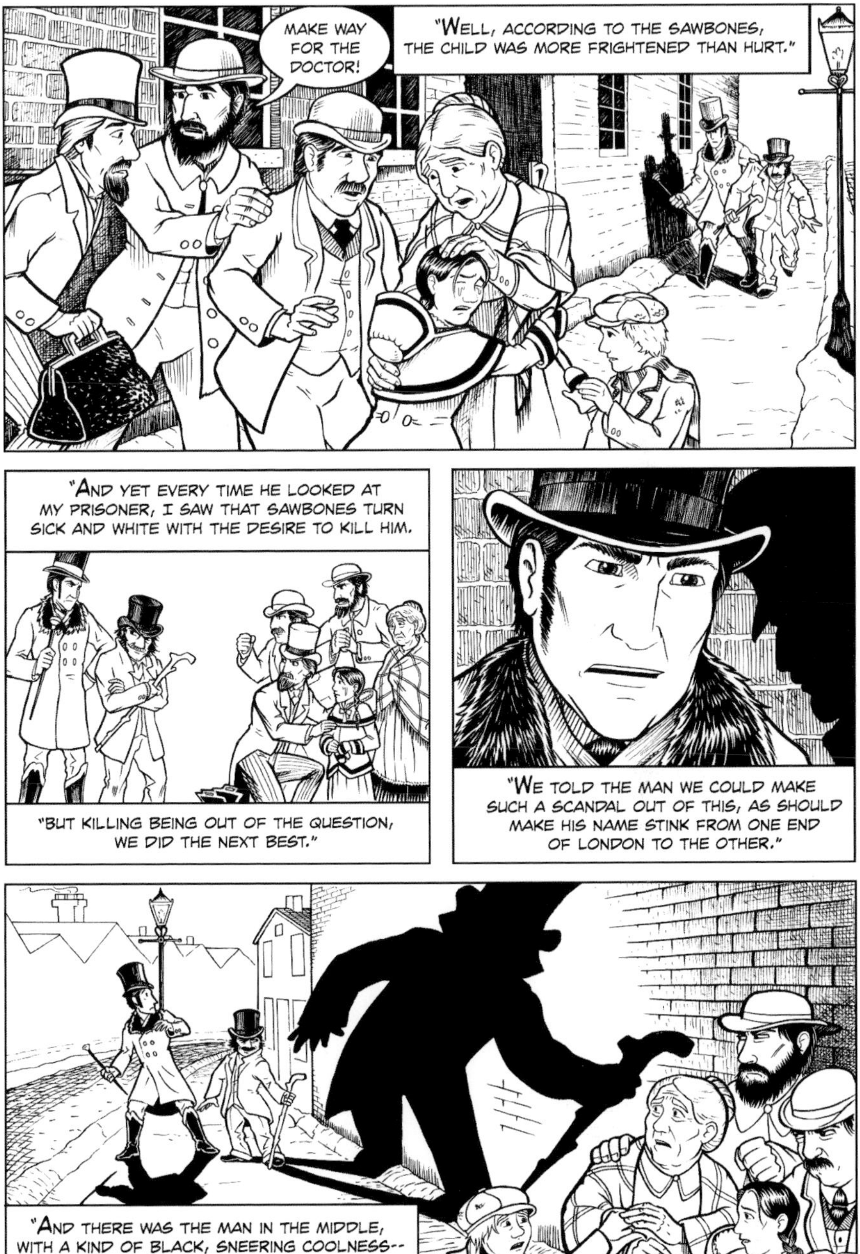

MAKE WAY FOR THE DOCTOR!
"WELL, ACCORDING TO THE SAWBONES, THE CHILD WAS MORE FRIGHTENED THAN HURT."
"AND YET EVERY TIME HE LOOKED AT MY PRISONER, I SAW THAT SAWBONES TURN SICK AND WHITE WITH THE DESIRE TO KILL HIM.
"BUT KILLING BEING OUT OF THE QUESTION, WE DID THE NEXT BEST."
"WE TOLD THE MAN WE COULD MAKE SUCH A SCANDAL OUT OF THIS, AS SHOULD MAKE HIS NAME STINK FROM ONE END OF LONDON TO THE OTHER."
"AND THERE WAS THE MAN IN THE MIDDLE, WITH A KIND OF BLACK, SNEERING COOLNESS-- FRIGHTENED TOO, I COULD SEE THAT-- BUT CARRYING IT OFF, REALLY LIKE SATAN."

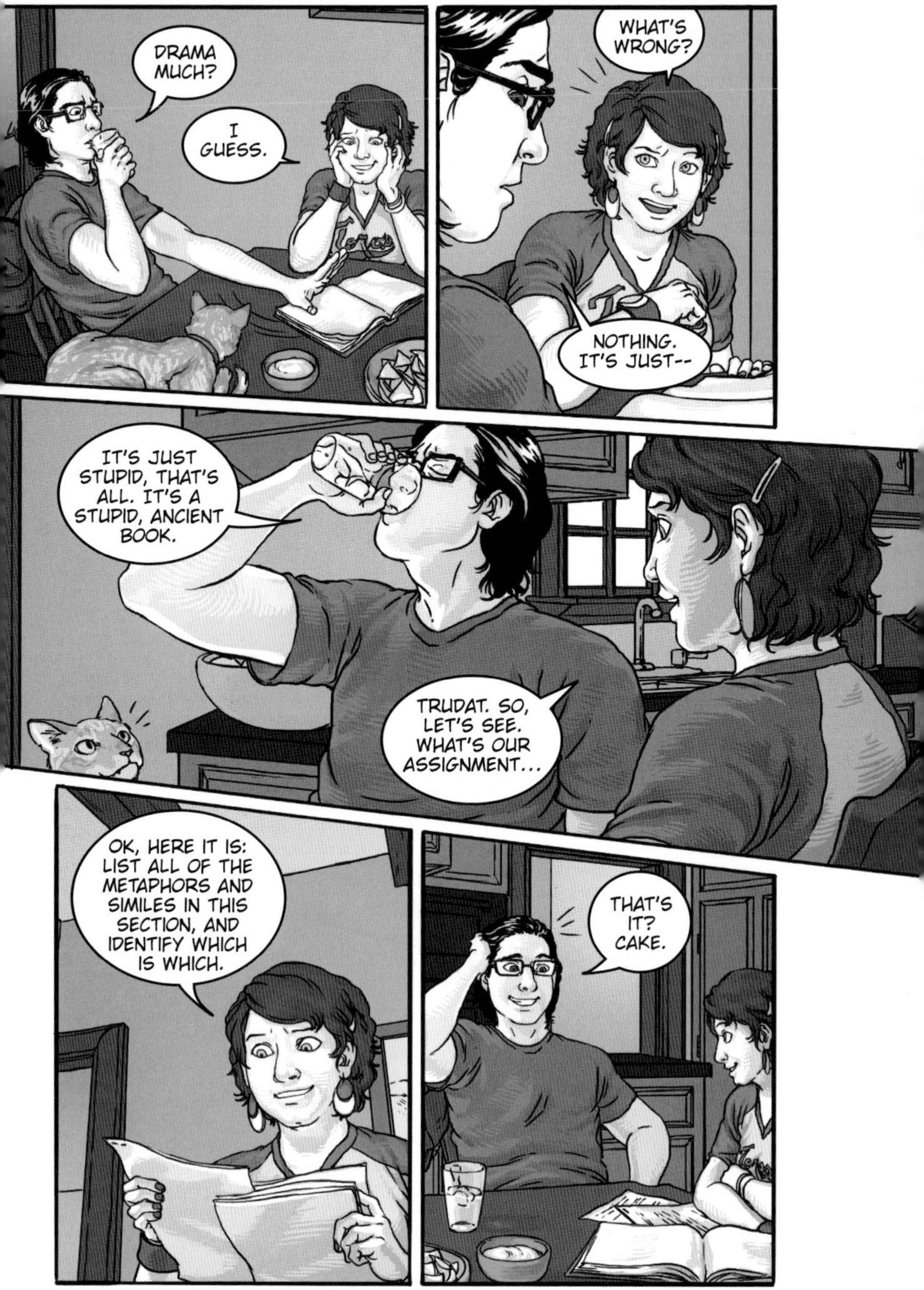
DRAMA MUCH?
I GUESS.
WHAT'S WRONG?
NOTHING. IT'S JUST--
IT'S JUST STUPID, THAT'S ALL. IT'S A STUPID, ANCIENT BOOK.
TRUDAT. SO, LET'S SEE. WHAT'S OUR ASSIGNMENT...
OK, HERE IT IS: LIST ALL OF THE METAPHORS AND SIMILES IN THIS SECTION, AND IDENTIFY WHICH IS WHICH.
THAT'S IT? CAKE.

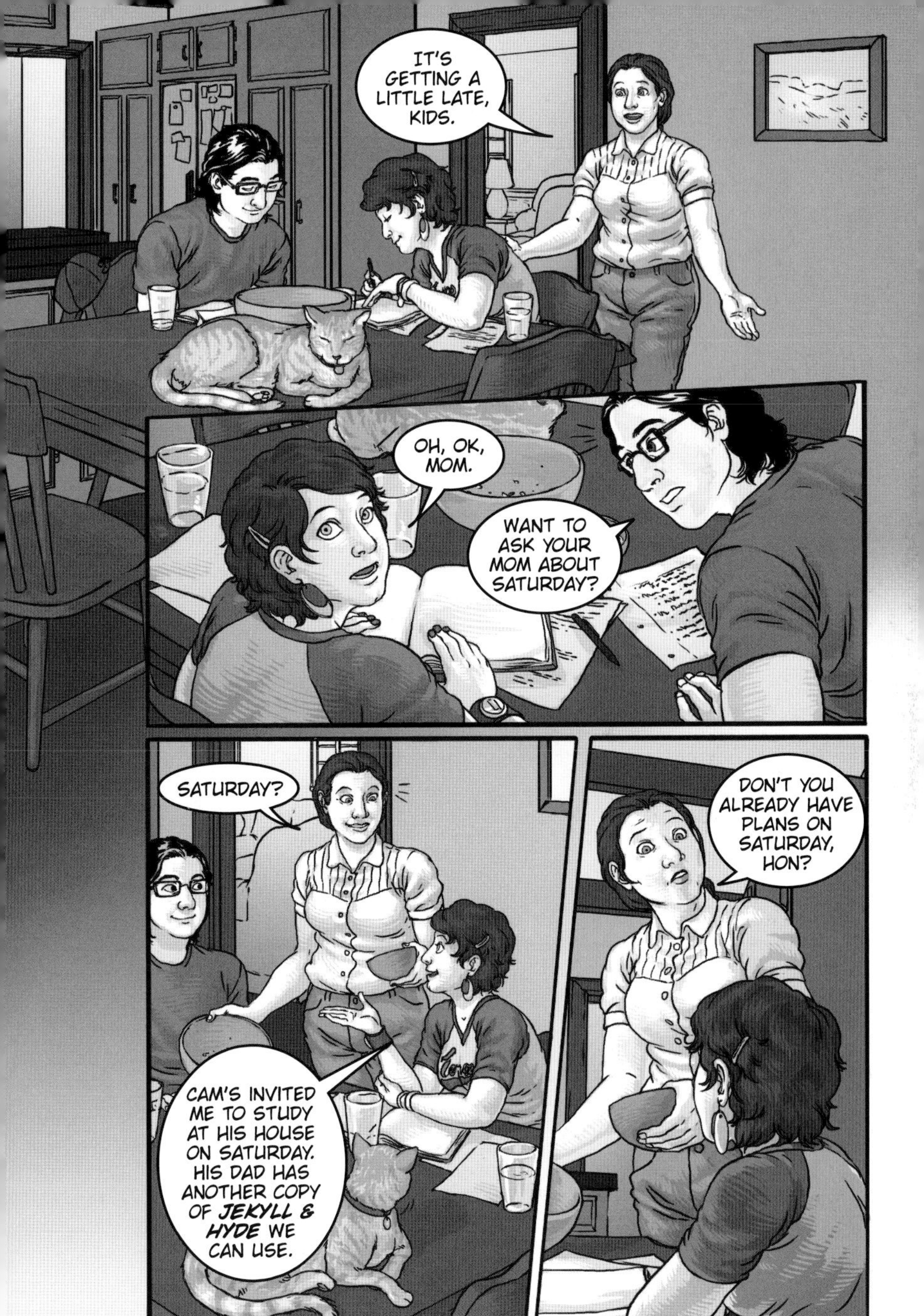
IT'S GETTING A LITTLE LATE, KIDS.
OH, OK, MOM.
WANT TO ASK YOUR MOM ABOUT SATURDAY?
SATURDAY?
CAM'S INVITED ME TO STUDY AT HIS HOUSE ON SATURDAY. HIS DAD HAS ANOTHER COPY OF *JEKYLL & HYDE* WE CAN USE.
DON'T YOU ALREADY HAVE PLANS ON SATURDAY, HON?

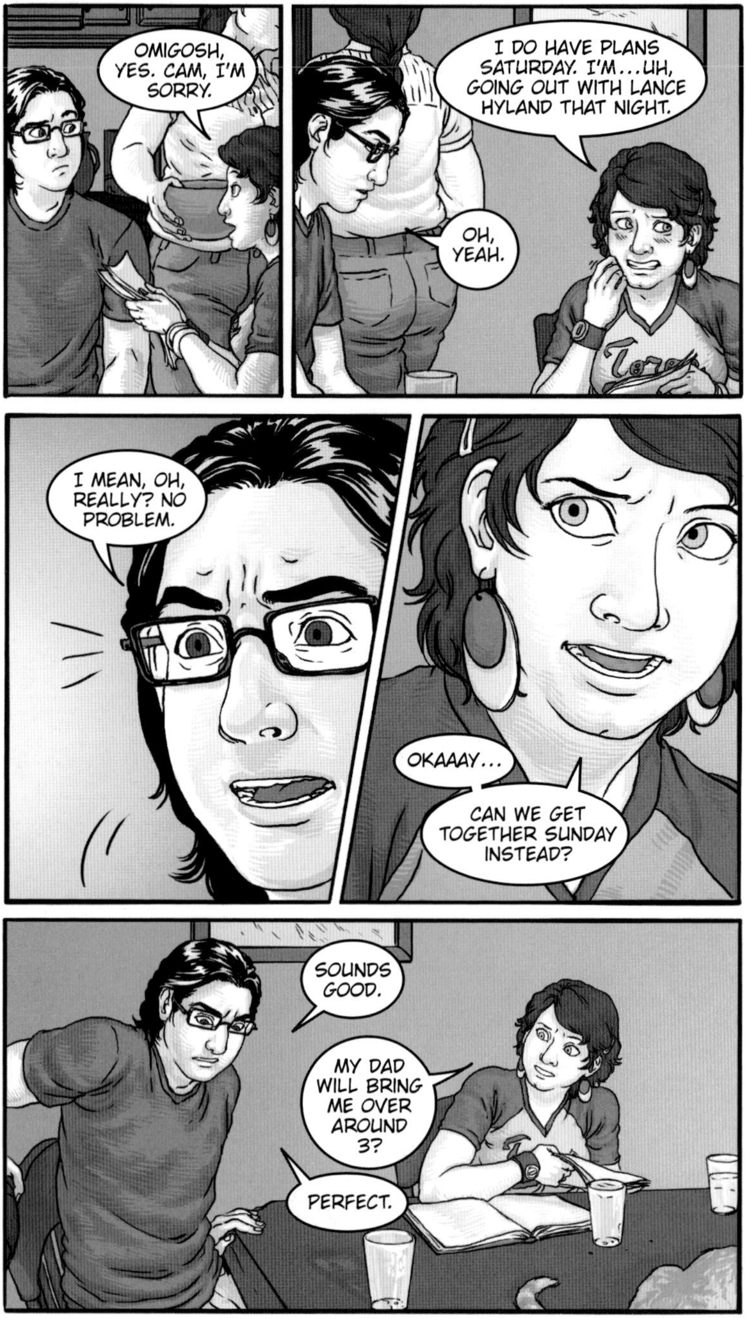
OMIGOSH, YES. CAM, I'M SORRY.
I DO HAVE PLANS SATURDAY. I'M...UH, GOING OUT WITH LANCE HYLAND THAT NIGHT.
OH, YEAH.
I MEAN, OH, REALLY? NO PROBLEM.
OKAAAY...
CAN WE GET TOGETHER SUNDAY INSTEAD?
SOUNDS GOOD.
MY DAD WILL BRING ME OVER AROUND 3?
PERFECT.

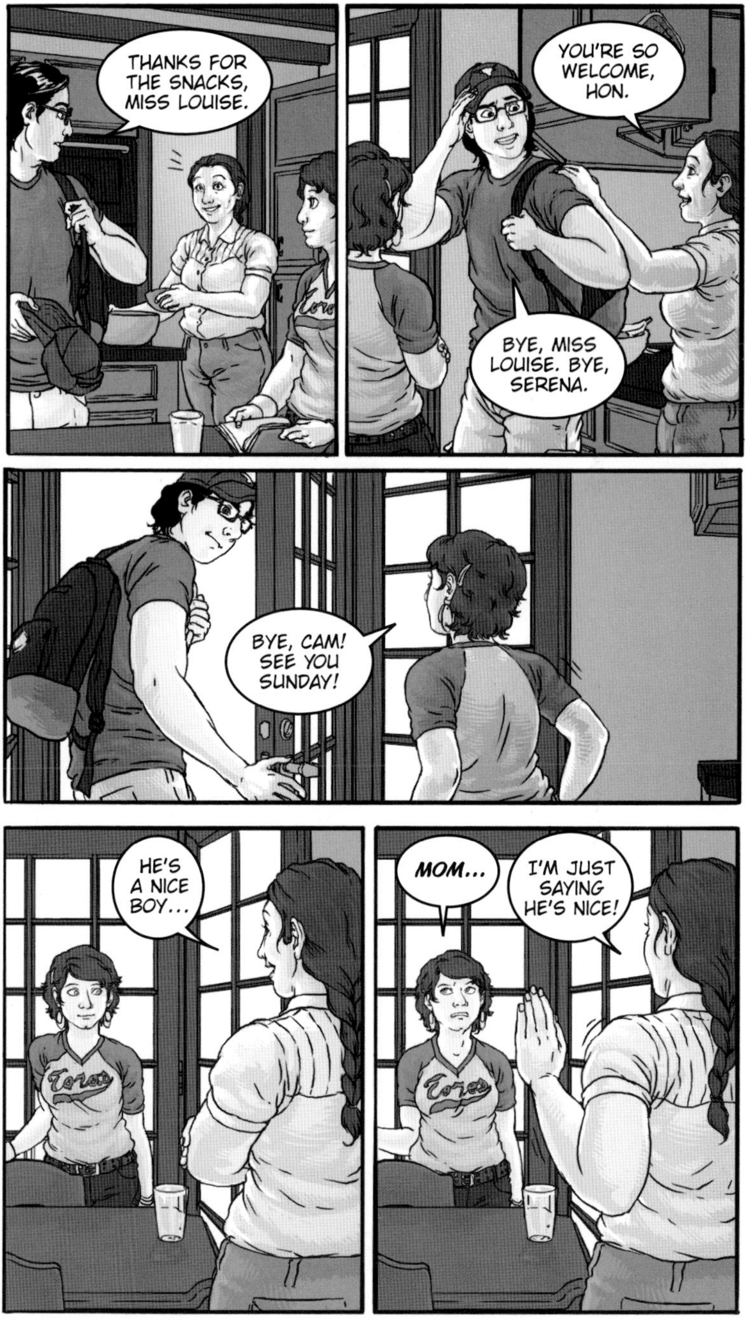
THANKS FOR THE SNACKS, MISS LOUISE.
YOU'RE SO WELCOME, HON.
BYE, MISS LOUISE. BYE, SERENA.
BYE, CAM! SEE YOU SUNDAY!
HE'S A NICE BOY...
MOM...
I'M JUST SAYING HE'S NICE!

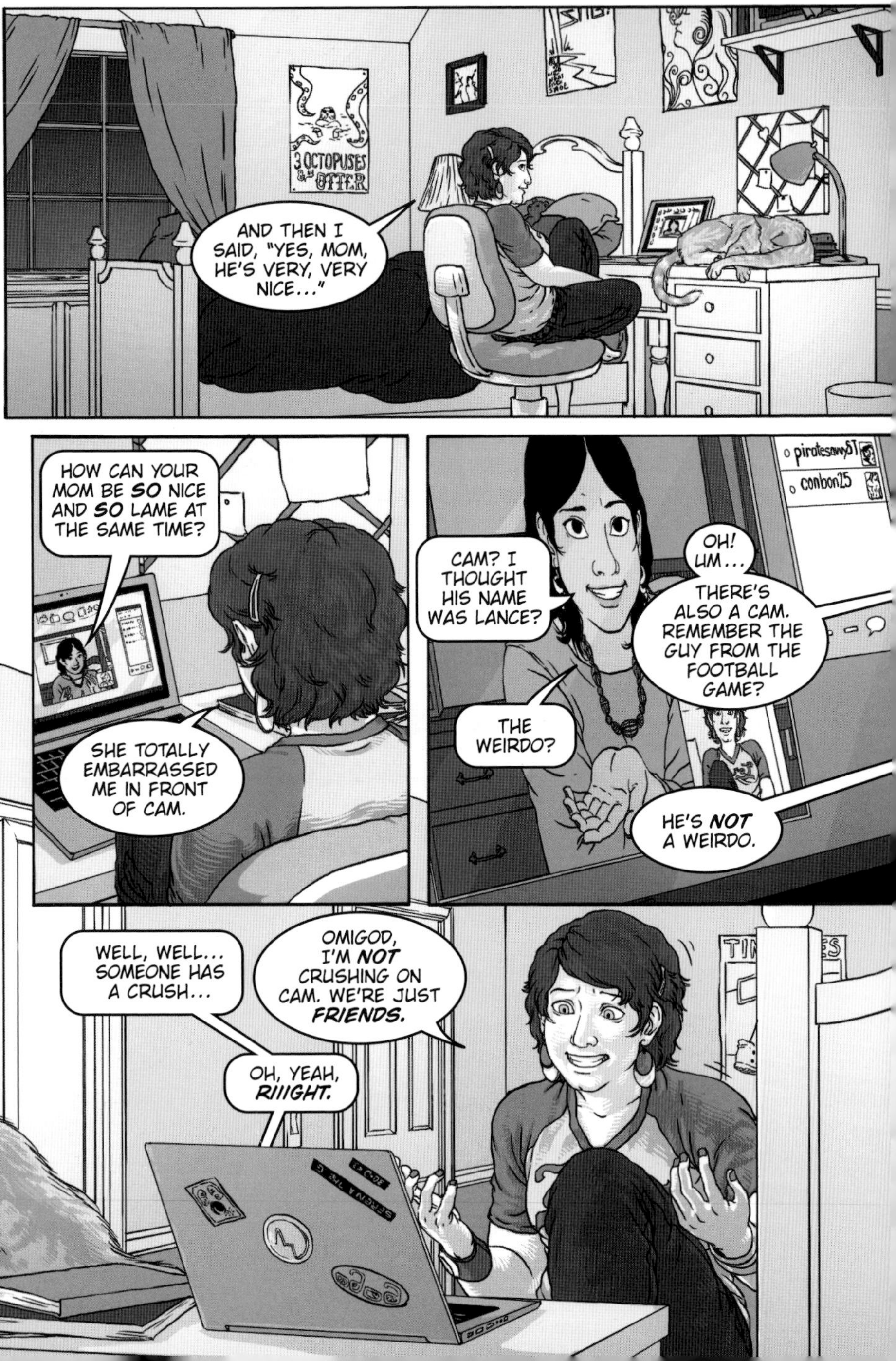
3 OCTOPUSES & AN OTTER
AND THEN I SAID, "YES, MOM, HE'S VERY, VERY NICE..."
HOW CAN YOUR MOM BE **SO** NICE AND **SO** LAME AT THE SAME TIME?
SHE TOTALLY EMBARRASSED ME IN FRONT OF CAM.
piratesavvyST
conbon25
CAM? I THOUGHT HIS NAME WAS LANCE?
OH! UM...
THERE'S ALSO A CAM. REMEMBER THE GUY FROM THE FOOTBALL GAME?
THE WEIRDO?
HE'S ***NOT*** A WEIRDO.
WELL, WELL... SOMEONE HAS A CRUSH...
OMIGOD, I'M ***NOT*** CRUSHING ON CAM. WE'RE JUST ***FRIENDS.***
OH, YEAH, ***RIIIGHT.***

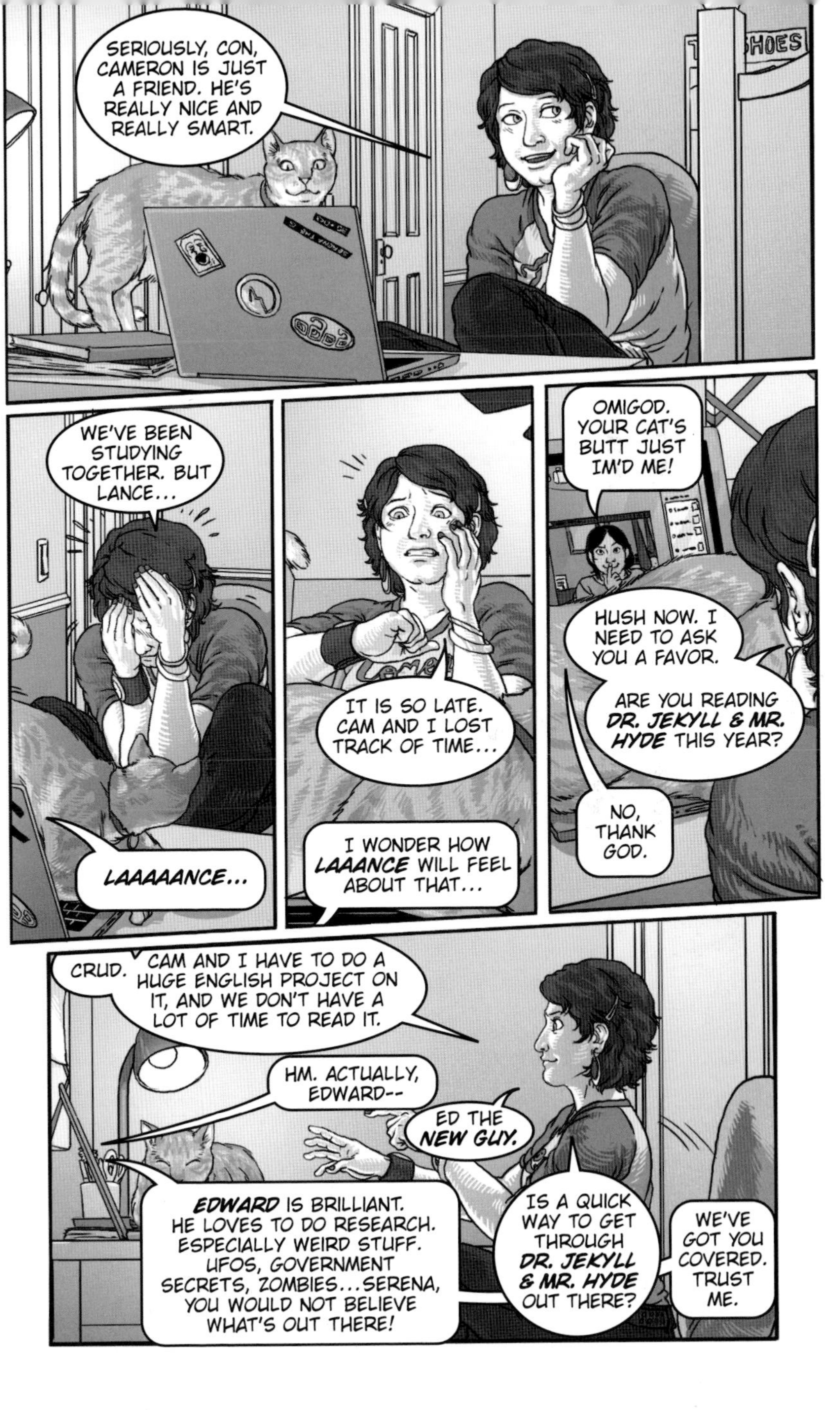
SERIOUSLY, CON, CAMERON IS JUST A FRIEND. HE'S REALLY NICE AND REALLY SMART.
SHOES
WE'VE BEEN STUDYING TOGETHER. BUT LANCE...
LAAAAANCE...
IT IS SO LATE. CAM AND I LOST TRACK OF TIME...
I WONDER HOW **LAAANCE** WILL FEEL ABOUT THAT...
OMIGOD. YOUR CAT'S BUTT JUST IM'D ME!
HUSH NOW. I NEED TO ASK YOU A FAVOR.
ARE YOU READING ***DR. JEKYLL & MR. HYDE*** THIS YEAR?
NO, THANK GOD.
CRUD.
CAM AND I HAVE TO DO A HUGE ENGLISH PROJECT ON IT, AND WE DON'T HAVE A LOT OF TIME TO READ IT.
HM. ACTUALLY, EDWARD--
ED THE ***NEW GUY.***
EDWARD IS BRILLIANT. HE LOVES TO DO RESEARCH. ESPECIALLY WEIRD STUFF. UFOS, GOVERNMENT SECRETS, ZOMBIES...SERENA, YOU WOULD NOT BELIEVE WHAT'S OUT THERE!
IS A QUICK WAY TO GET THROUGH ***DR. JEKYLL & MR. HYDE*** OUT THERE?
WE'VE GOT YOU COVERED. TRUST ME.

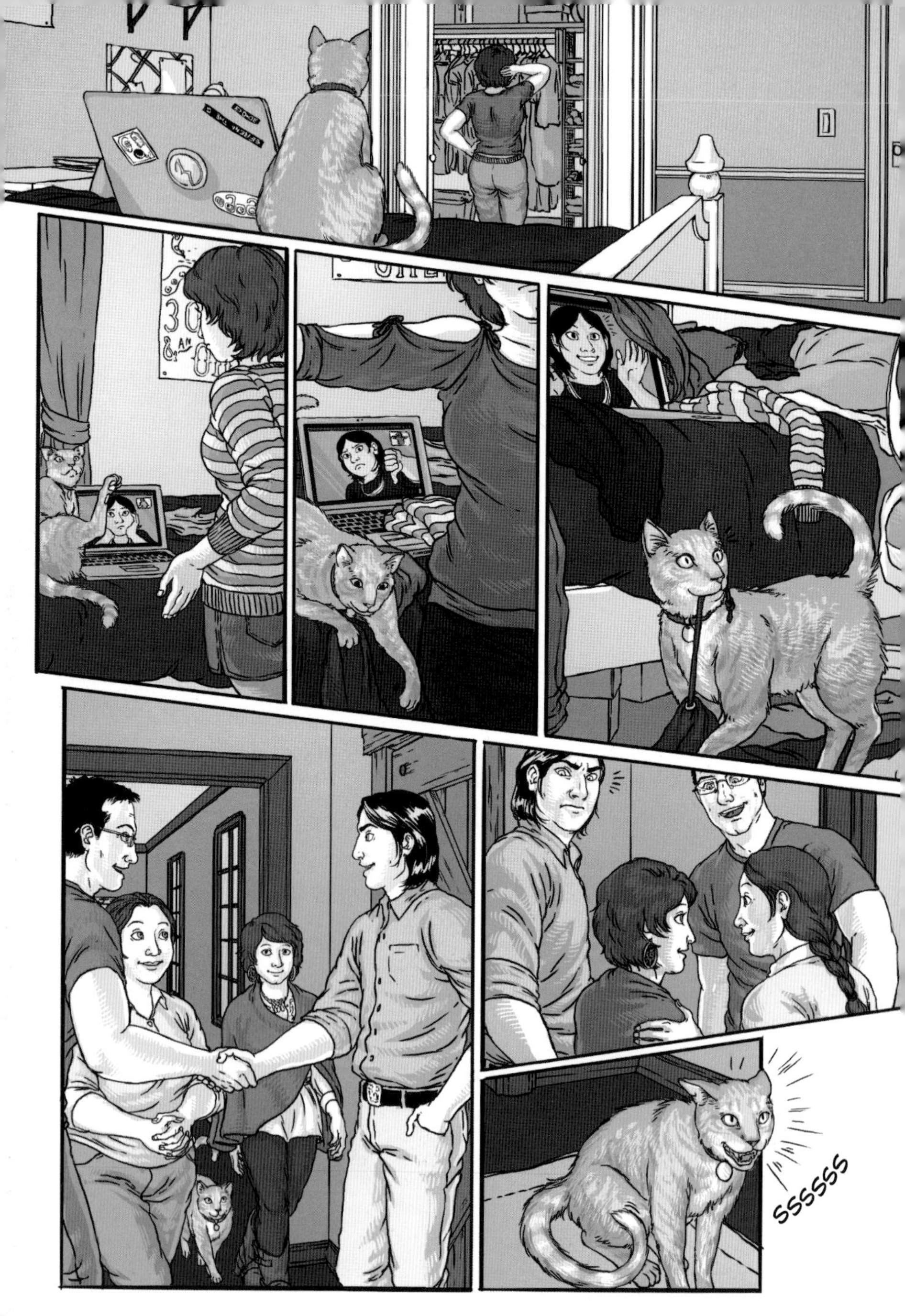
SSSSSS

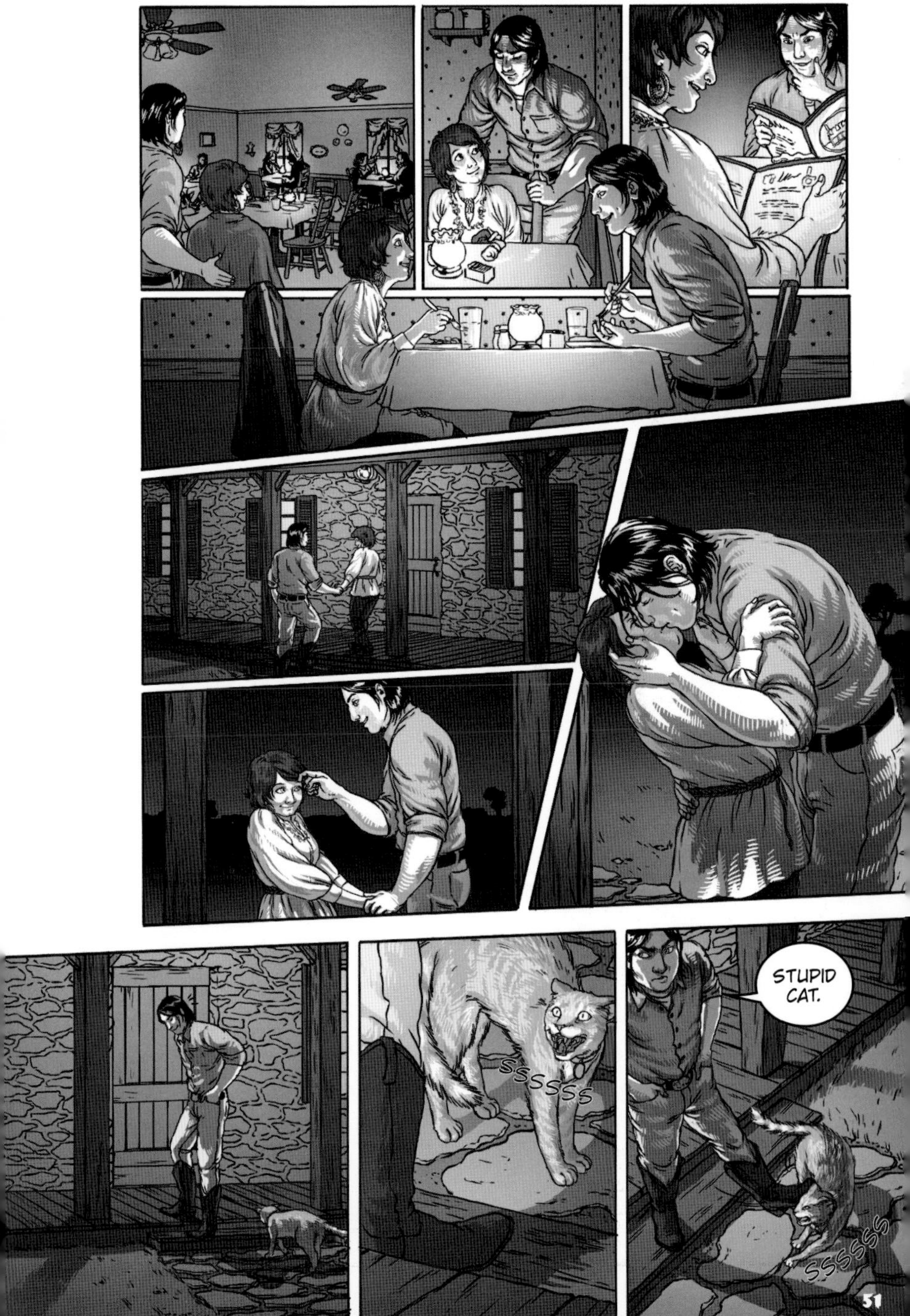
SSSSSS
STUPID CAT.
SSSSSS

Chapter FIVE
MYSTERIOUS WAYS

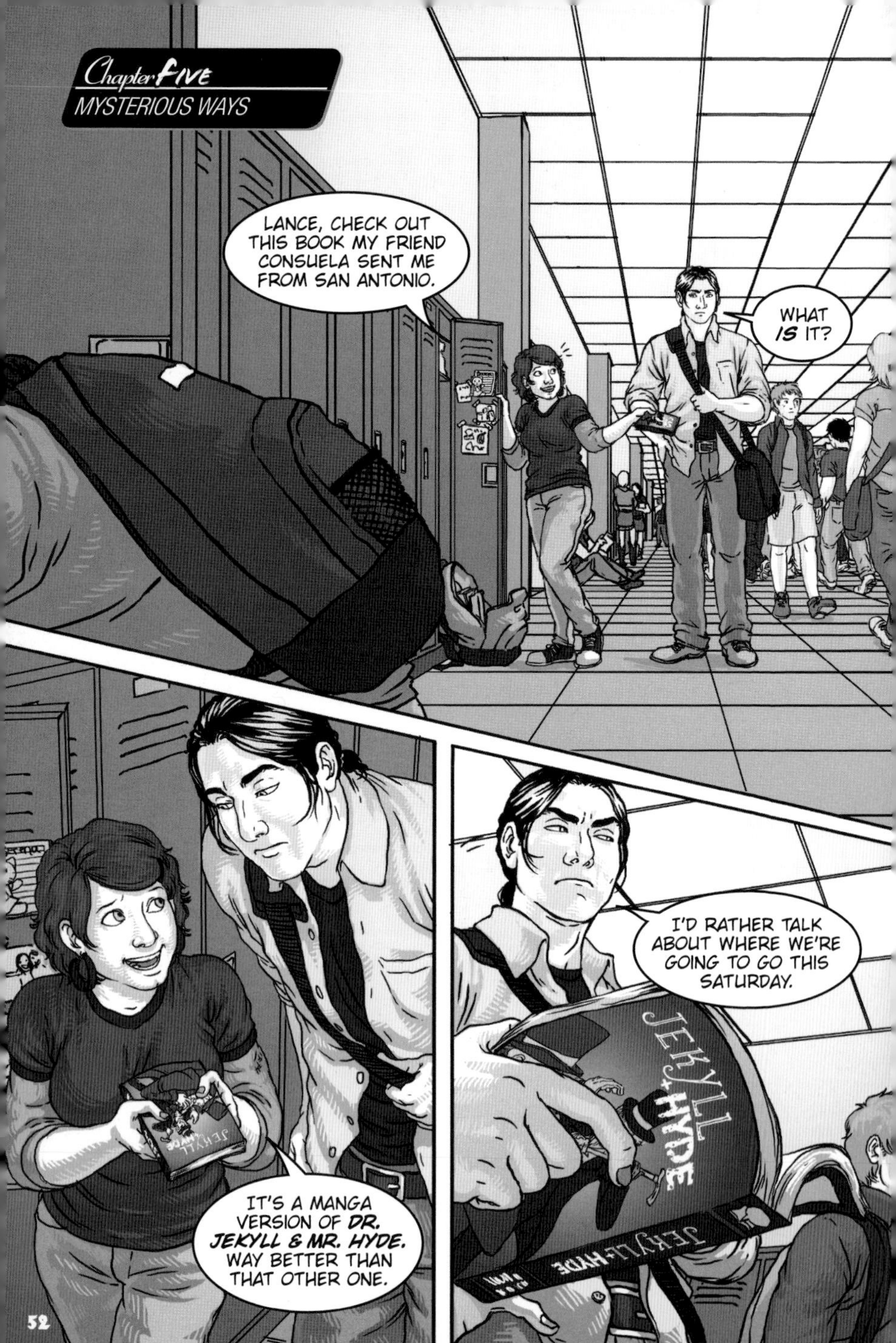

LANCE, CHECK OUT THIS BOOK MY FRIEND CONSUELA SENT ME FROM SAN ANTONIO.
WHAT *IS* IT?
IT'S A MANGA VERSION OF ***DR. JEKYLL & MR. HYDE.*** WAY BETTER THAN THAT OTHER ONE.
I'D RATHER TALK ABOUT WHERE WE'RE GOING TO GO THIS SATURDAY.
JEKYLL + HYDE

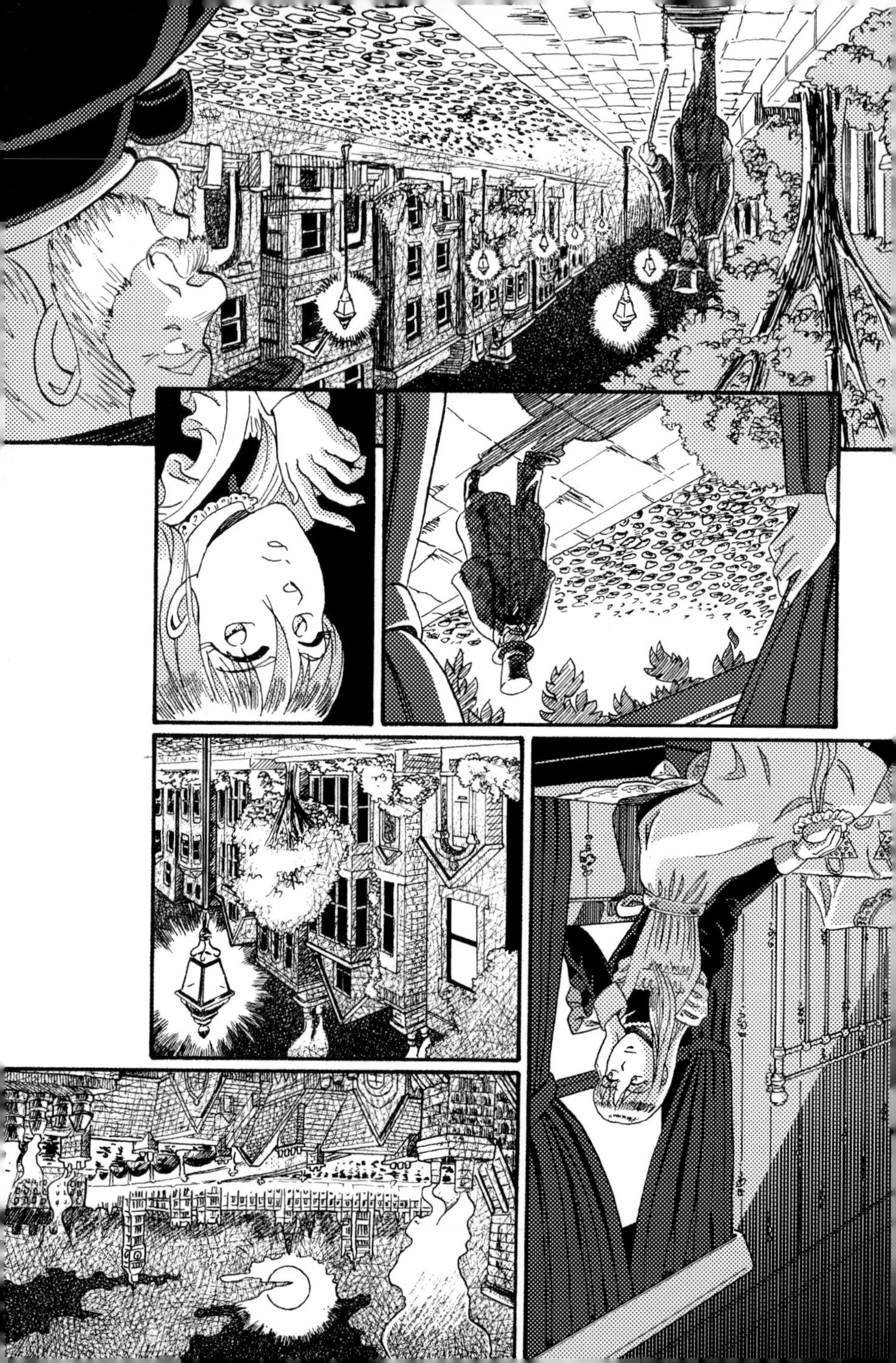

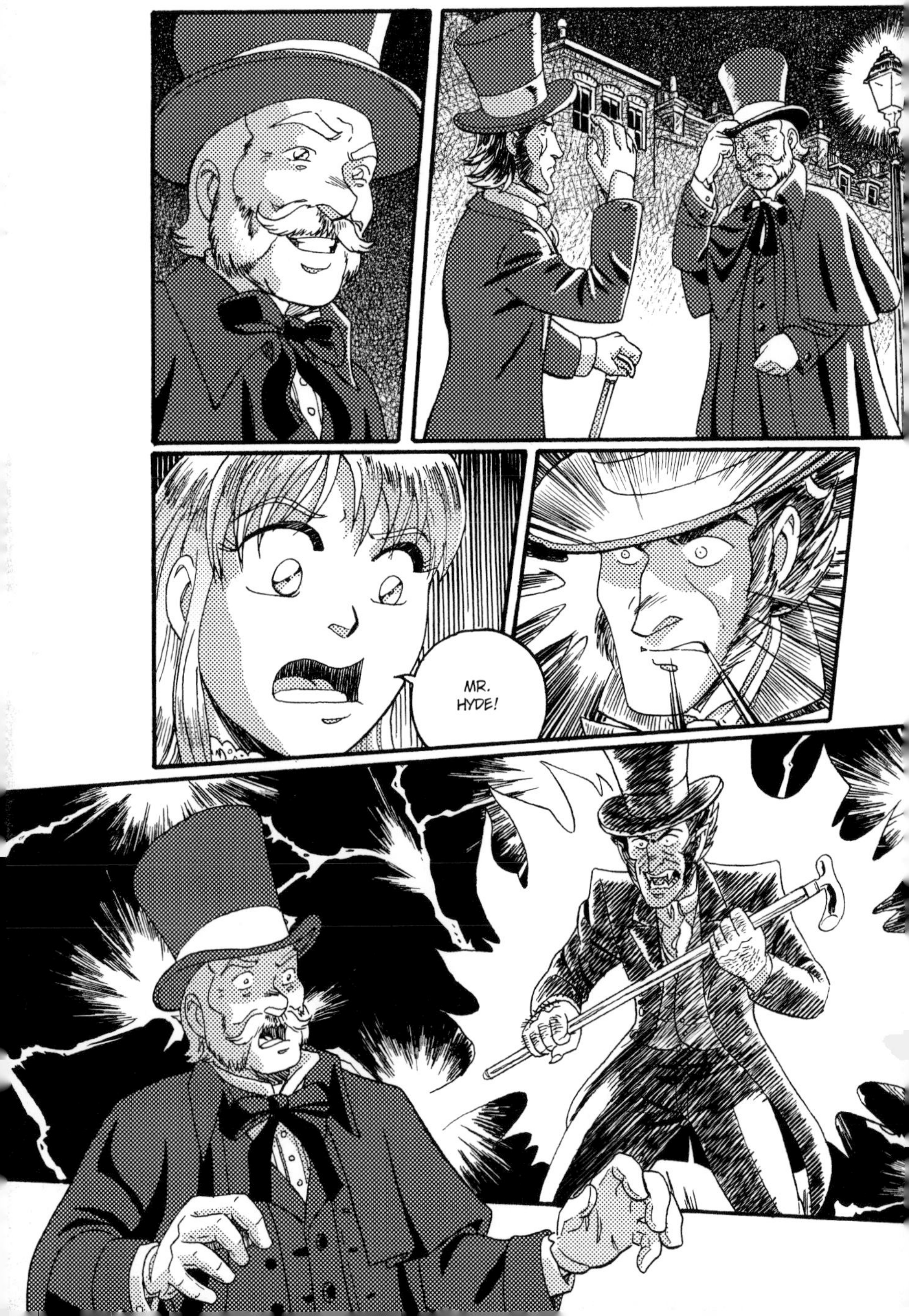
MR. HYDE!

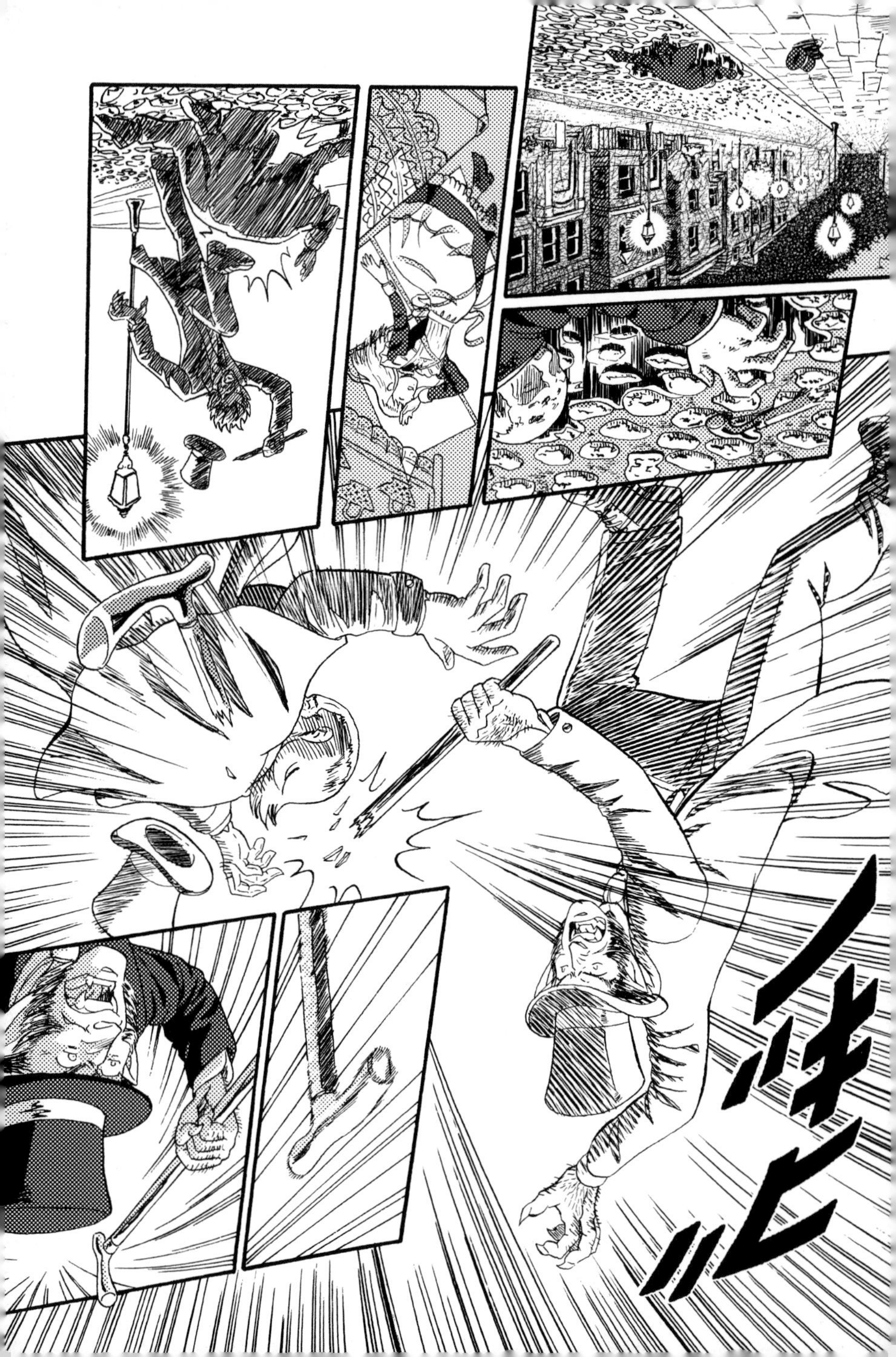

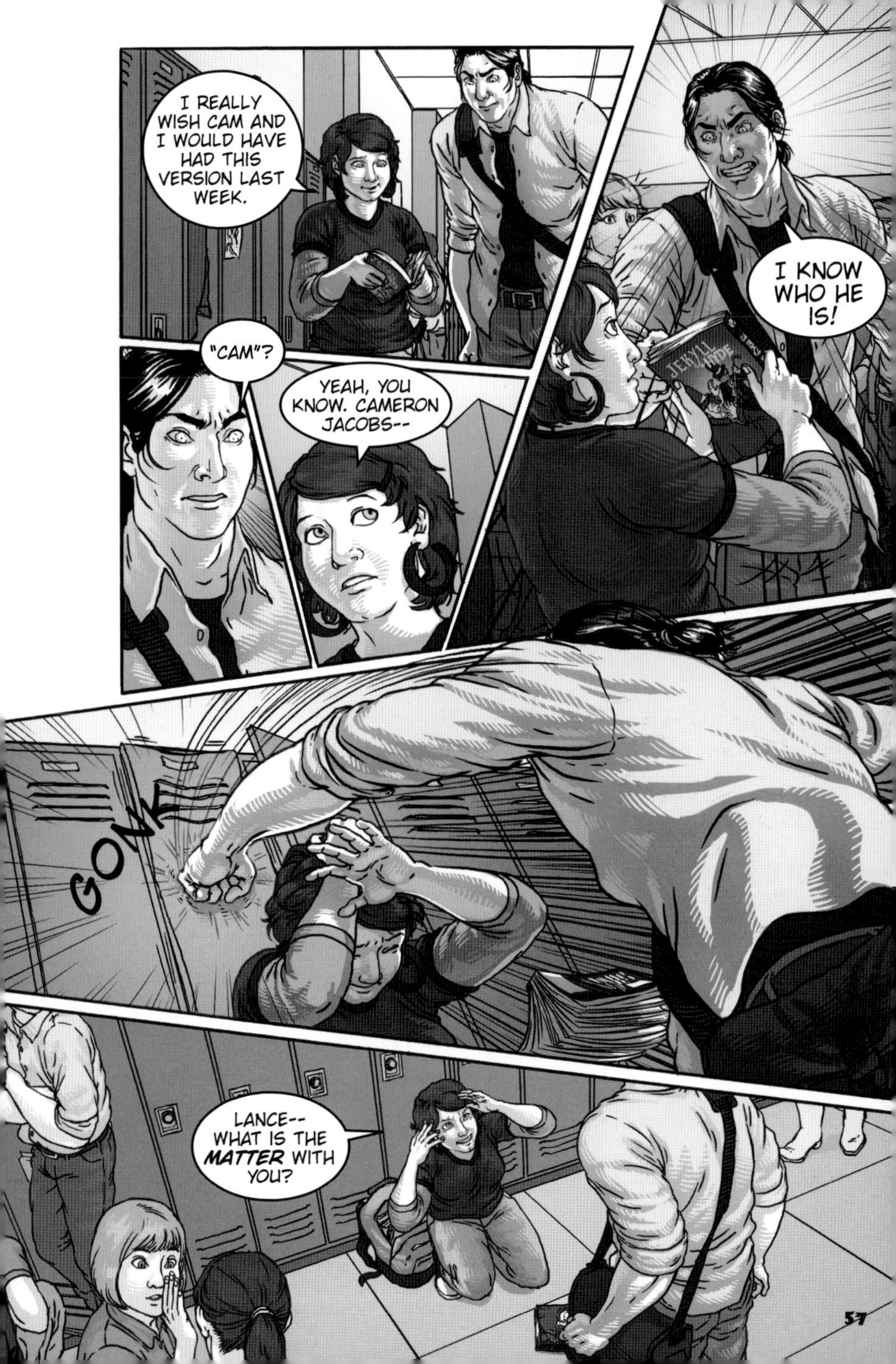

I REALLY WISH CAM AND I WOULD HAVE HAD THIS VERSION LAST WEEK.
"CAM"?
YEAH, YOU KNOW. CAMERON JACOBS--
I KNOW WHO HE IS!
JEKYLL HYDE
GONK
LANCE-- WHAT IS THE ***MATTER*** WITH YOU?

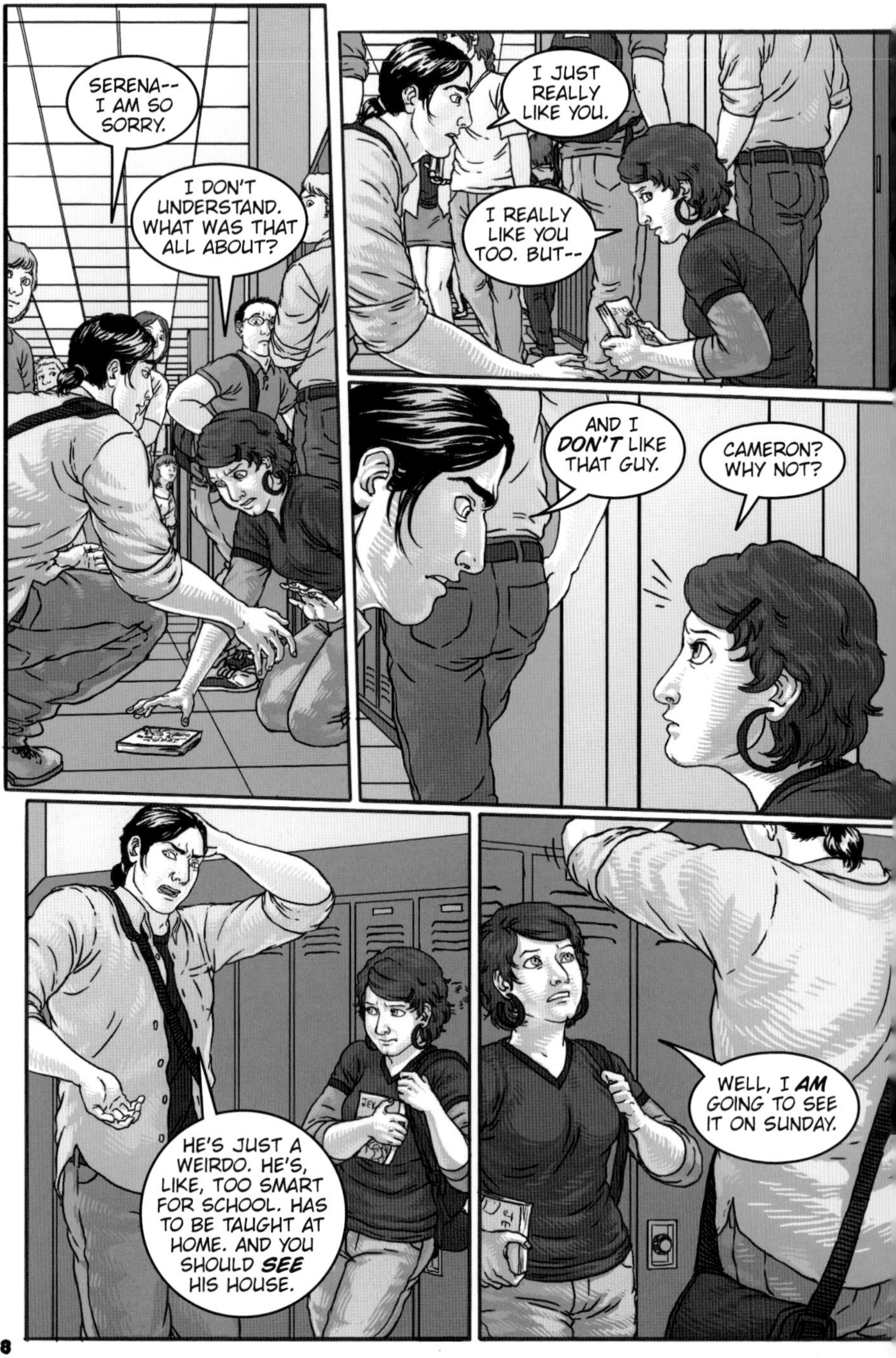
SERENA--
I AM SO
SORRY.
I DON'T
UNDERSTAND.
WHAT WAS THAT
ALL ABOUT?
I JUST
REALLY
LIKE YOU.
I REALLY
LIKE YOU
TOO. BUT--
AND I
DON'T LIKE
THAT GUY.
CAMERON?
WHY NOT?
HE'S JUST A
WEIRDO. HE'S,
LIKE, TOO SMART
FOR SCHOOL. HAS
TO BE TAUGHT AT
HOME. AND YOU
SHOULD **SEE**
HIS HOUSE.
WELL, I **AM**
GOING TO SEE
IT ON SUNDAY.

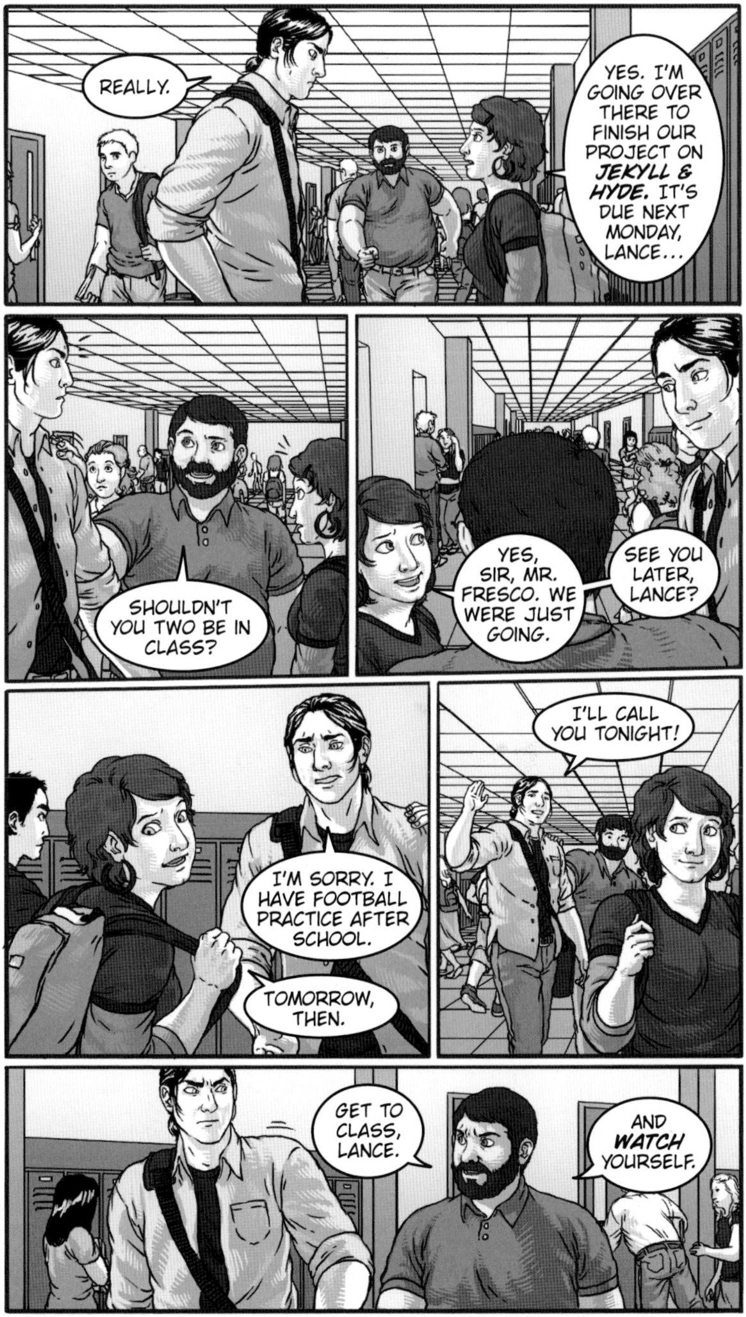
REALLY.
YES. I'M GOING OVER THERE TO FINISH OUR PROJECT ON ***JEKYLL & HYDE.*** IT'S DUE NEXT MONDAY, LANCE...
SHOULDN'T YOU TWO BE IN CLASS?
YES, SIR, MR. FRESCO. WE WERE JUST GOING.
SEE YOU LATER, LANCE?
I'M SORRY. I HAVE FOOTBALL PRACTICE AFTER SCHOOL.
TOMORROW, THEN.
I'LL CALL YOU TONIGHT!
GET TO CLASS, LANCE.
AND ***WATCH*** YOURSELF.

Chapter SIX
OMG, It's FRIDAY

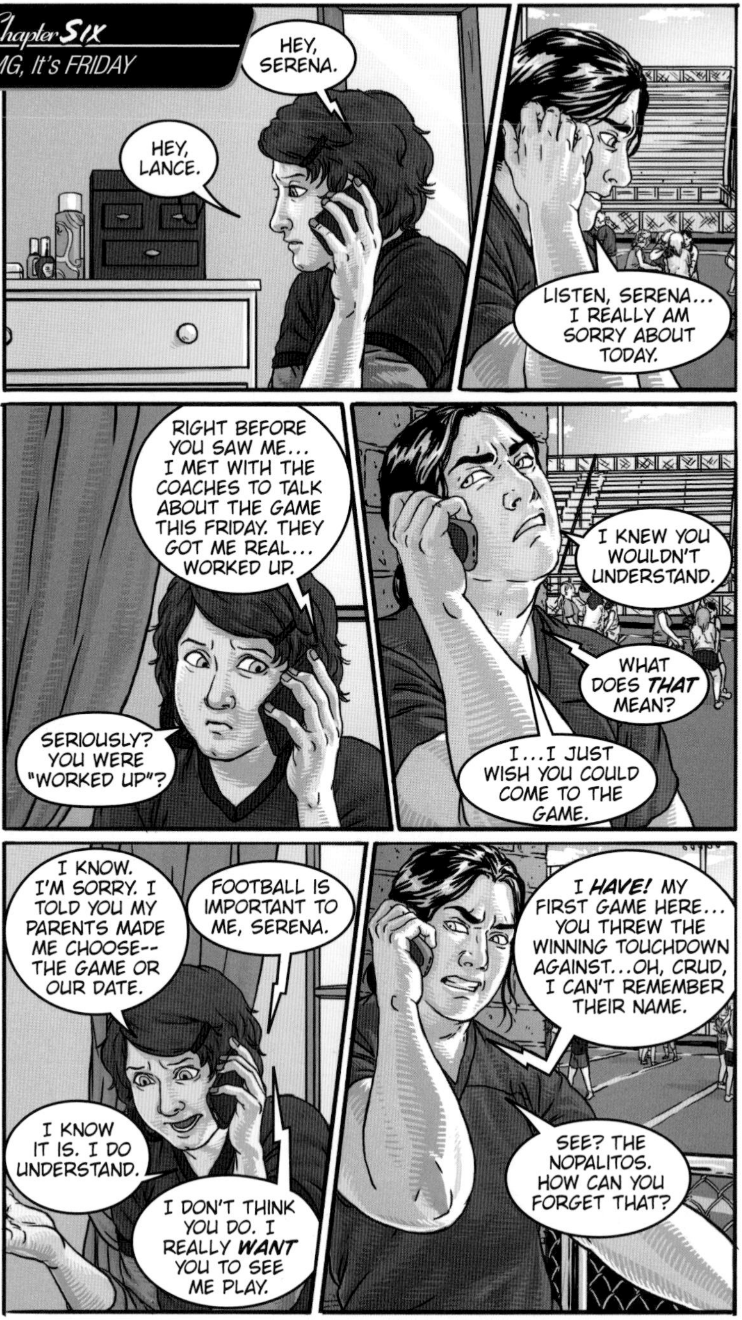
HEY, SERENA.
HEY, LANCE.
LISTEN, SERENA... I REALLY AM SORRY ABOUT TODAY.
RIGHT BEFORE YOU SAW ME... I MET WITH THE COACHES TO TALK ABOUT THE GAME THIS FRIDAY. THEY GOT ME REAL... WORKED UP.
SERIOUSLY? YOU WERE "WORKED UP"?
I KNEW YOU WOULDN'T UNDERSTAND.
WHAT DOES THAT MEAN?
I...I JUST WISH YOU COULD COME TO THE GAME.
I KNOW. I'M SORRY. I TOLD YOU MY PARENTS MADE ME CHOOSE-- THE GAME OR OUR DATE.
FOOTBALL IS IMPORTANT TO ME, SERENA.
I KNOW IT IS. I DO UNDERSTAND.
I DON'T THINK YOU DO. I REALLY WANT YOU TO SEE ME PLAY.
I HAVE! MY FIRST GAME HERE... YOU THREW THE WINNING TOUCHDOWN AGAINST...OH, CRUD, I CAN'T REMEMBER THEIR NAME.
SEE? THE NOPALITOS. HOW CAN YOU FORGET THAT?

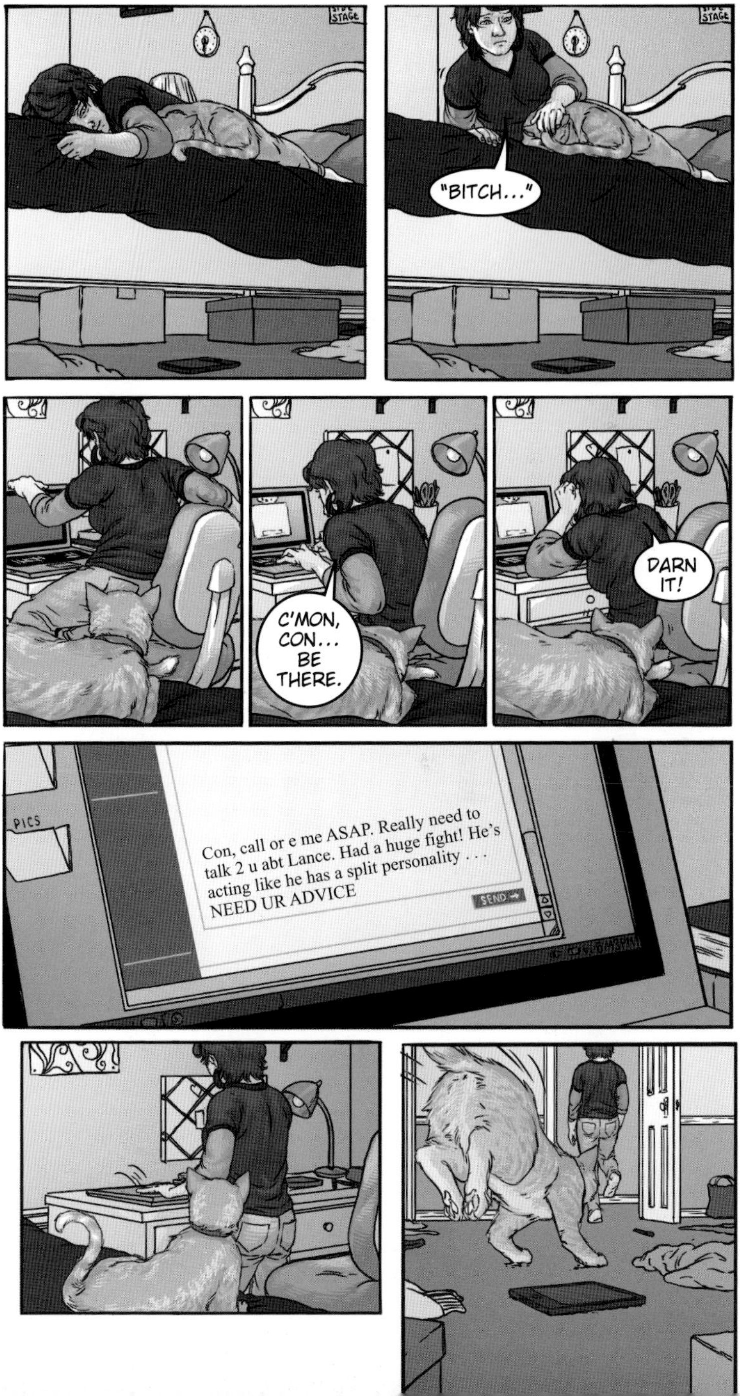
STAGE
STAGE
"BITCH..."
C'MON, CON... BE THERE.
DARN IT!
PICS
Con, call or e me ASAP. Really need to talk 2 u abt Lance. Had a huge fight! He's acting like he has a split personality . . . NEED UR ADVICE
SEND

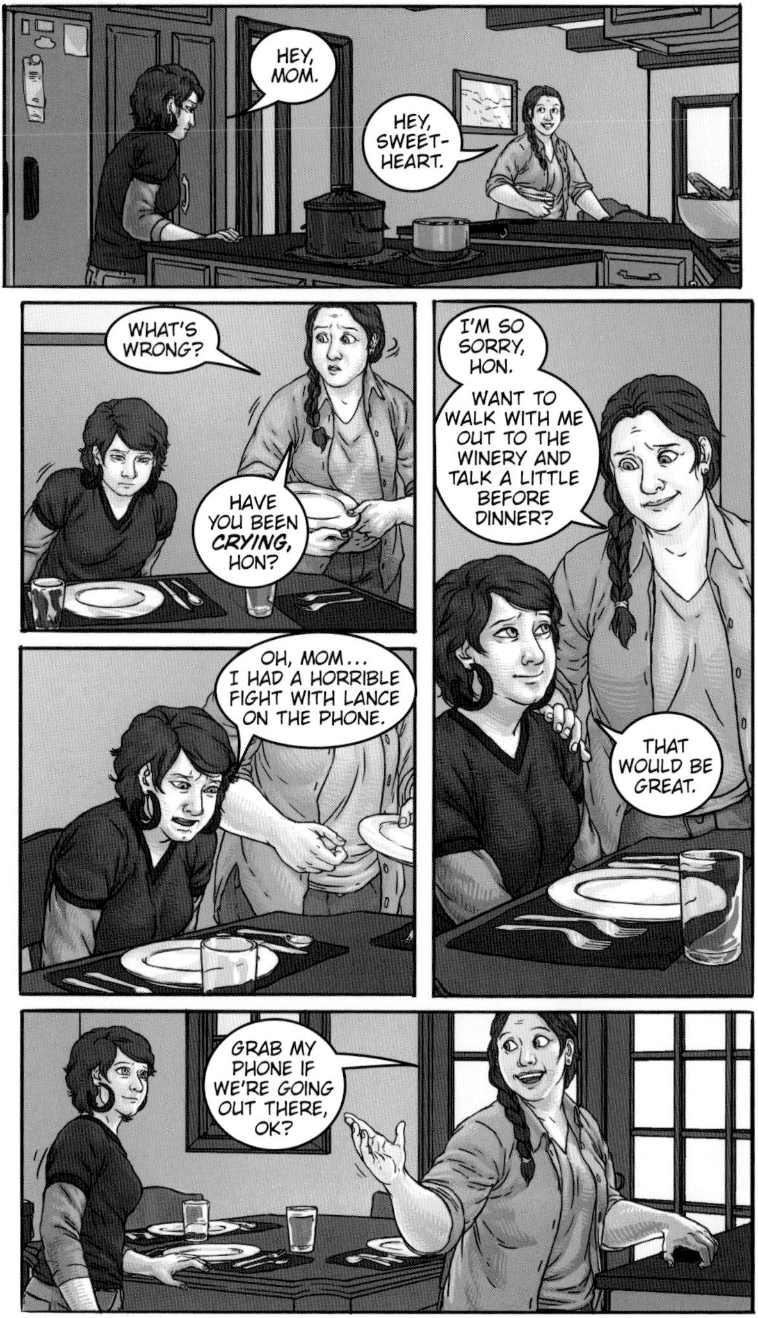
HEY, MOM.
HEY, SWEET-HEART.
WHAT'S WRONG?
HAVE YOU BEEN *CRYING,* HON?
OH, MOM... I HAD A HORRIBLE FIGHT WITH LANCE ON THE PHONE.
I'M SO SORRY, HON.
WANT TO WALK WITH ME OUT TO THE WINERY AND TALK A LITTLE BEFORE DINNER?
THAT WOULD BE GREAT.
GRAB MY PHONE IF WE'RE GOING OUT THERE, OK?

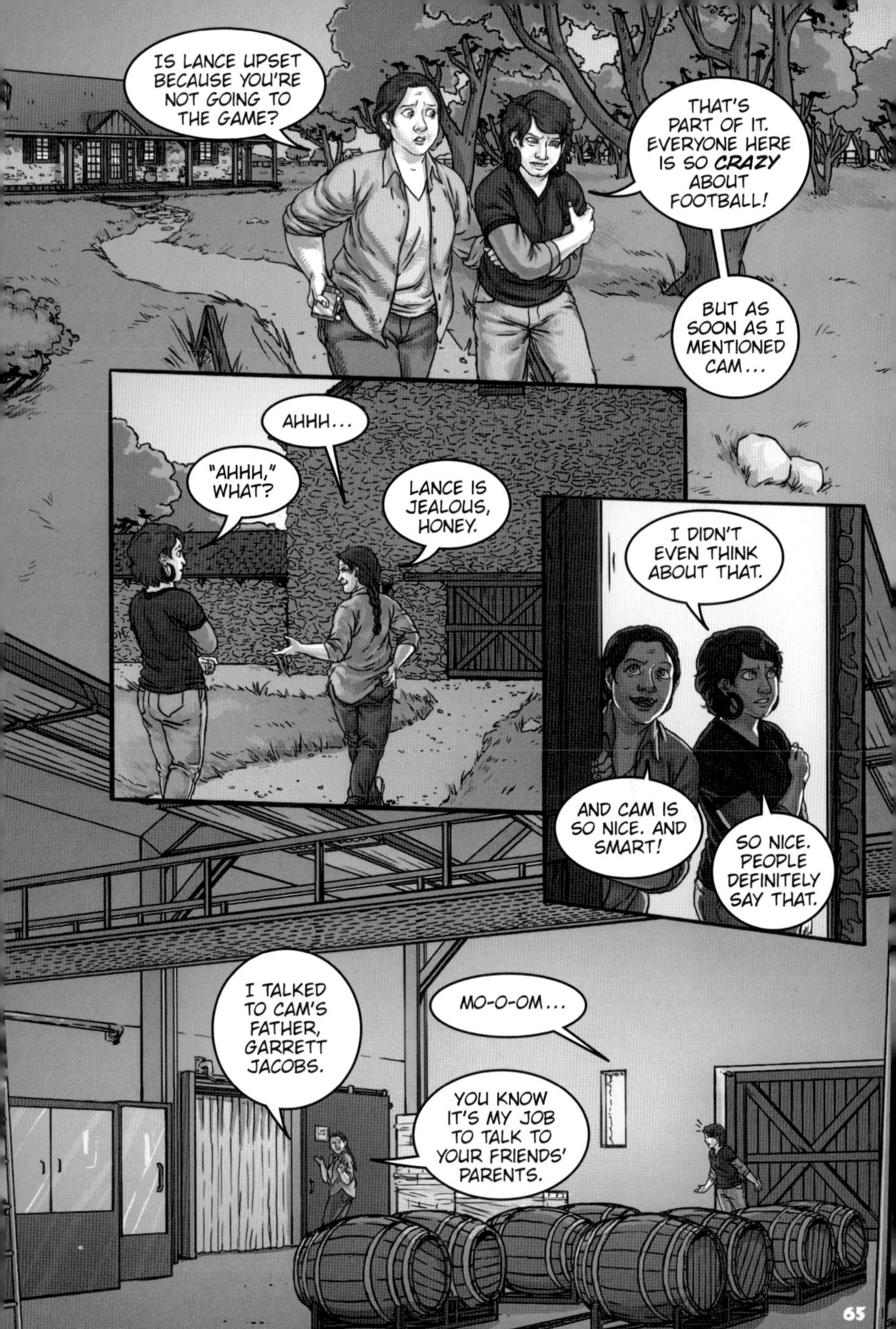
IS LANCE UPSET BECAUSE YOU'RE NOT GOING TO THE GAME?
THAT'S PART OF IT. EVERYONE HERE IS SO *CRAZY* ABOUT FOOTBALL!
BUT AS SOON AS I MENTIONED CAM...
AHHH...
"AHHH," WHAT?
LANCE IS JEALOUS, HONEY.
I DIDN'T EVEN THINK ABOUT THAT.
AND CAM IS SO NICE. AND SMART!
SO NICE. PEOPLE DEFINITELY SAY THAT.
I TALKED TO CAM'S FATHER, GARRETT JACOBS.
MO-O-OM...
YOU KNOW IT'S MY JOB TO TALK TO YOUR FRIENDS' PARENTS.

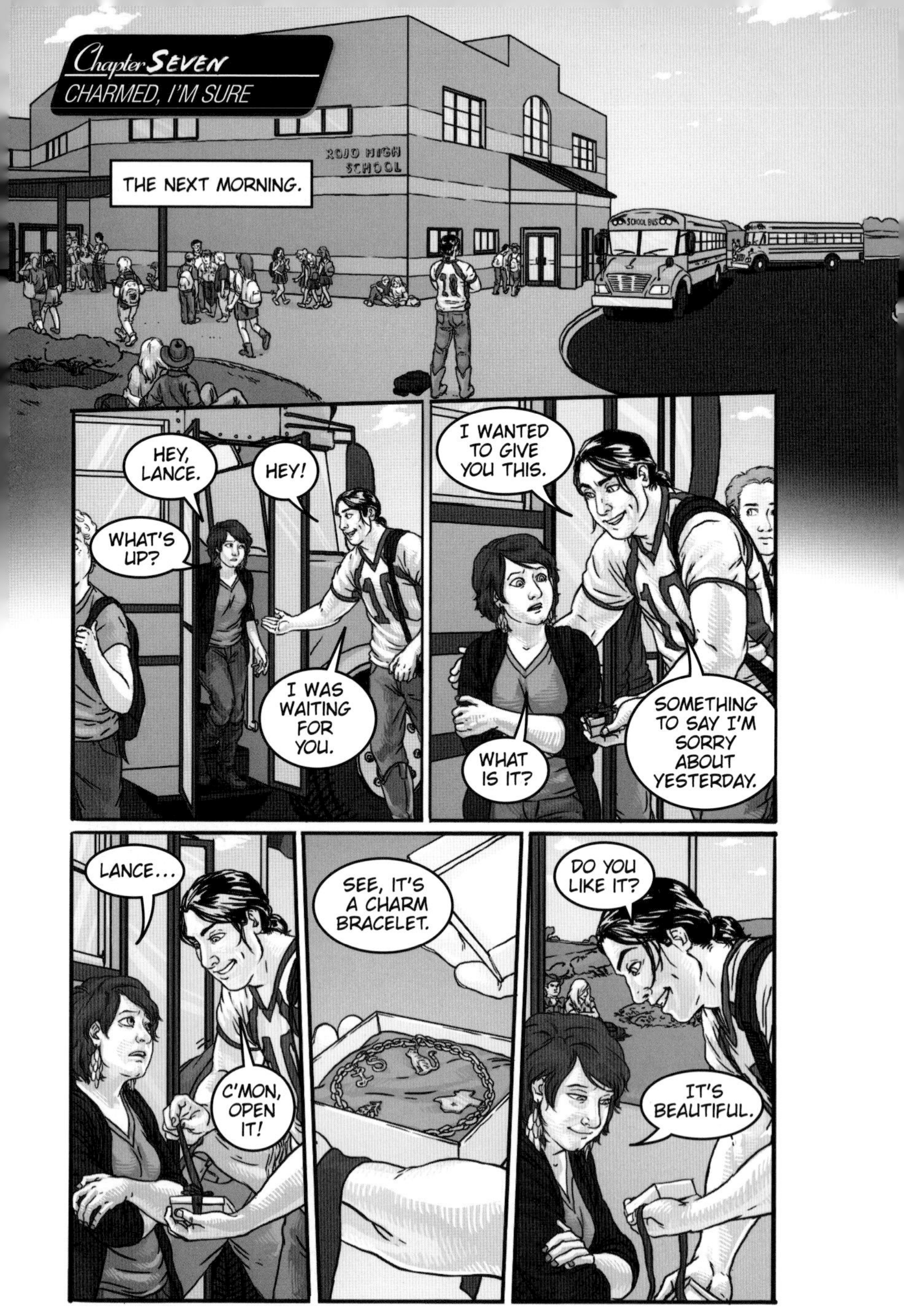
Chapter SEVEN
CHARMED, I'M SURE
ROJO HIGH SCHOOL
THE NEXT MORNING.
SCHOOL BUS
HEY, LANCE.
HEY!
WHAT'S UP?
I WAS WAITING FOR YOU.
I WANTED TO GIVE YOU THIS.
WHAT IS IT?
SOMETHING TO SAY I'M SORRY ABOUT YESTERDAY.
LANCE...
C'MON, OPEN IT!
SEE, IT'S A CHARM BRACELET.
DO YOU LIKE IT?
IT'S BEAUTIFUL.

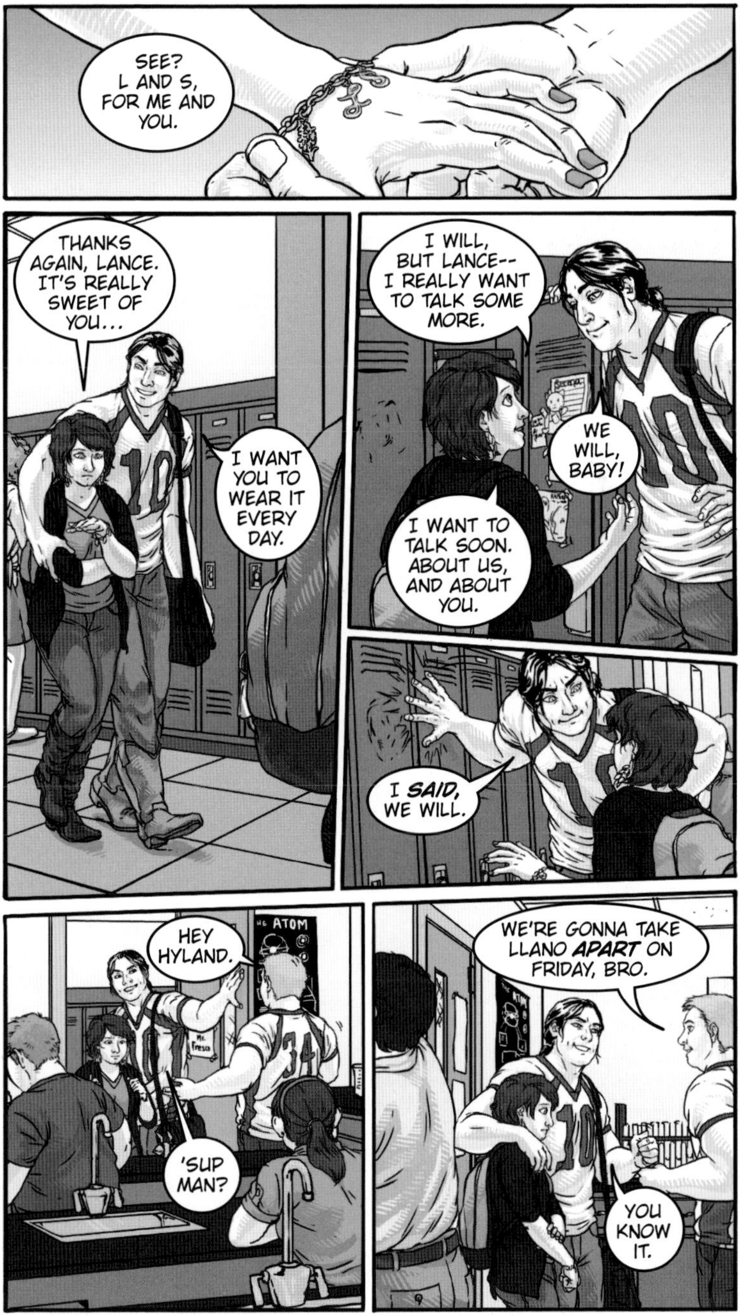
SEE? L AND S, FOR ME AND YOU.
THANKS AGAIN, LANCE. IT'S REALLY SWEET OF YOU...
I WANT YOU TO WEAR IT EVERY DAY.
I WILL, BUT LANCE-- I REALLY WANT TO TALK SOME MORE.
WE WILL, BABY!
I WANT TO TALK SOON. ABOUT US, AND ABOUT YOU.
I SAID, WE WILL.
HEY HYLAND.
'SUP MAN?
WE'RE GONNA TAKE LLANO APART ON FRIDAY, BRO.
YOU KNOW IT.

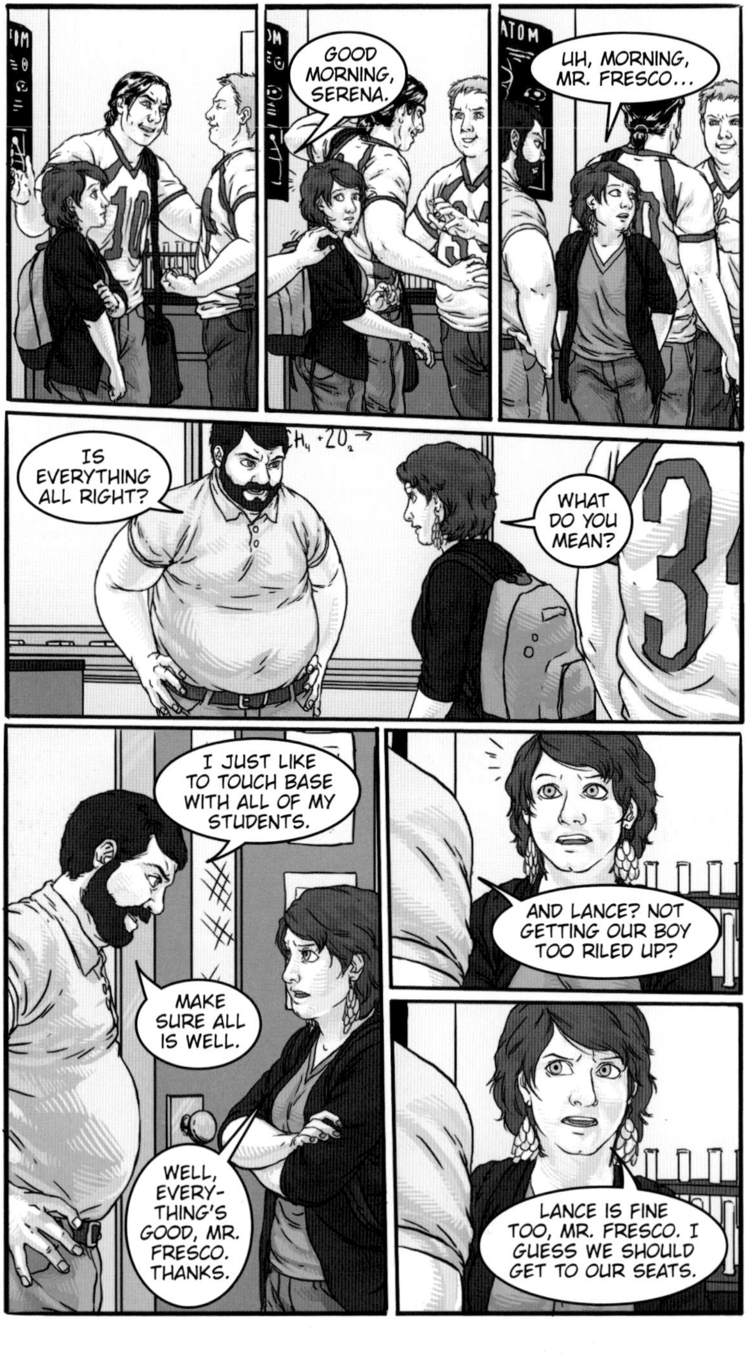
GOOD MORNING, SERENA.
UH, MORNING, MR. FRESCO...
IS EVERYTHING ALL RIGHT?
WHAT DO YOU MEAN?
I JUST LIKE TO TOUCH BASE WITH ALL OF MY STUDENTS.
MAKE SURE ALL IS WELL.
WELL, EVERY-THING'S GOOD, MR. FRESCO. THANKS.
AND LANCE? NOT GETTING OUR BOY TOO RILED UP?
LANCE IS FINE TOO, MR. FRESCO. I GUESS WE SHOULD GET TO OUR SEATS.

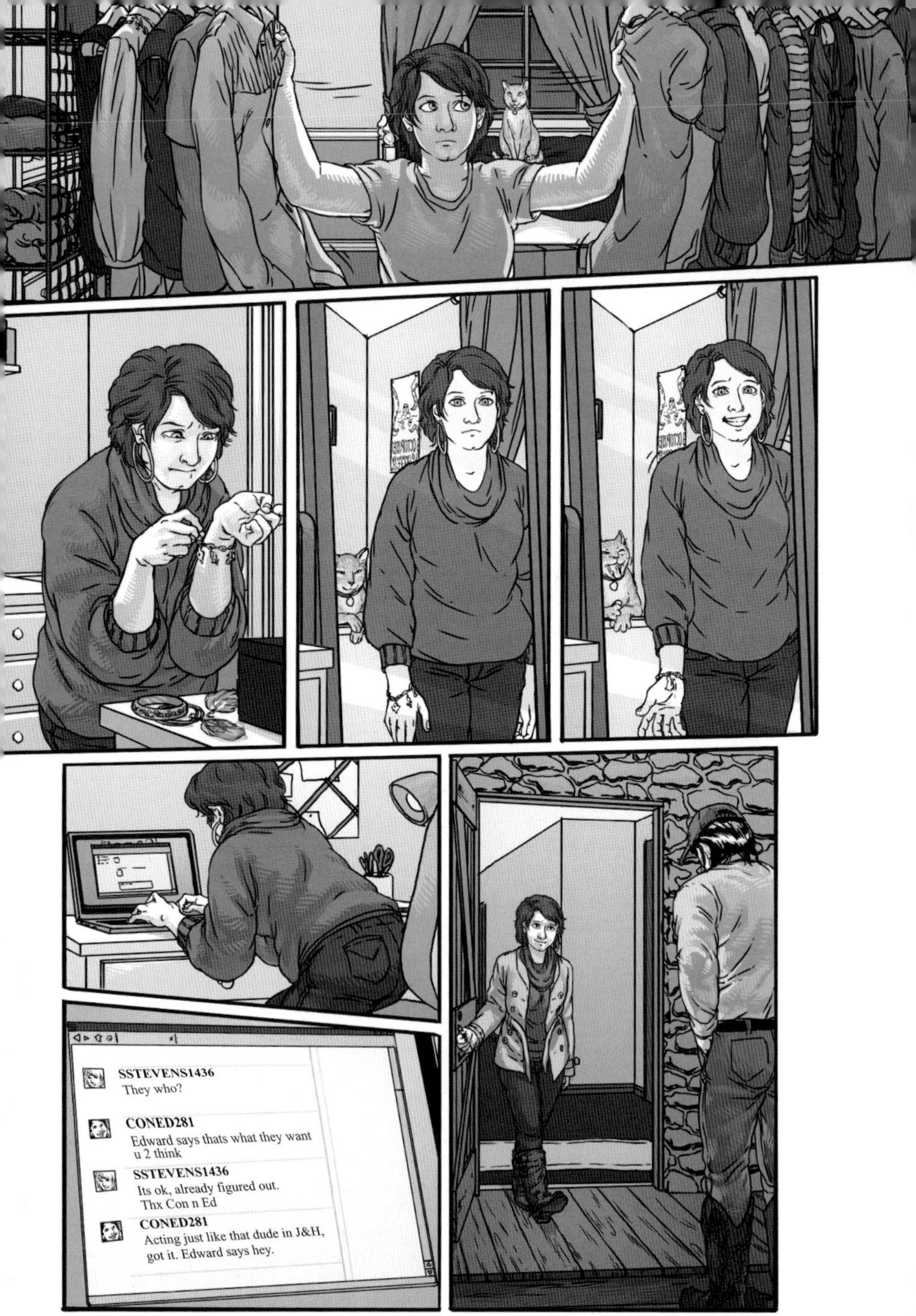
SSTEVENS1436
They who?
CONED281
Edward says thats what they want u 2 think
SSTEVENS1436
Its ok, already figured out. Thx Con n Ed
CONED281
Acting just like that dude in J&H, got it. Edward says hey.

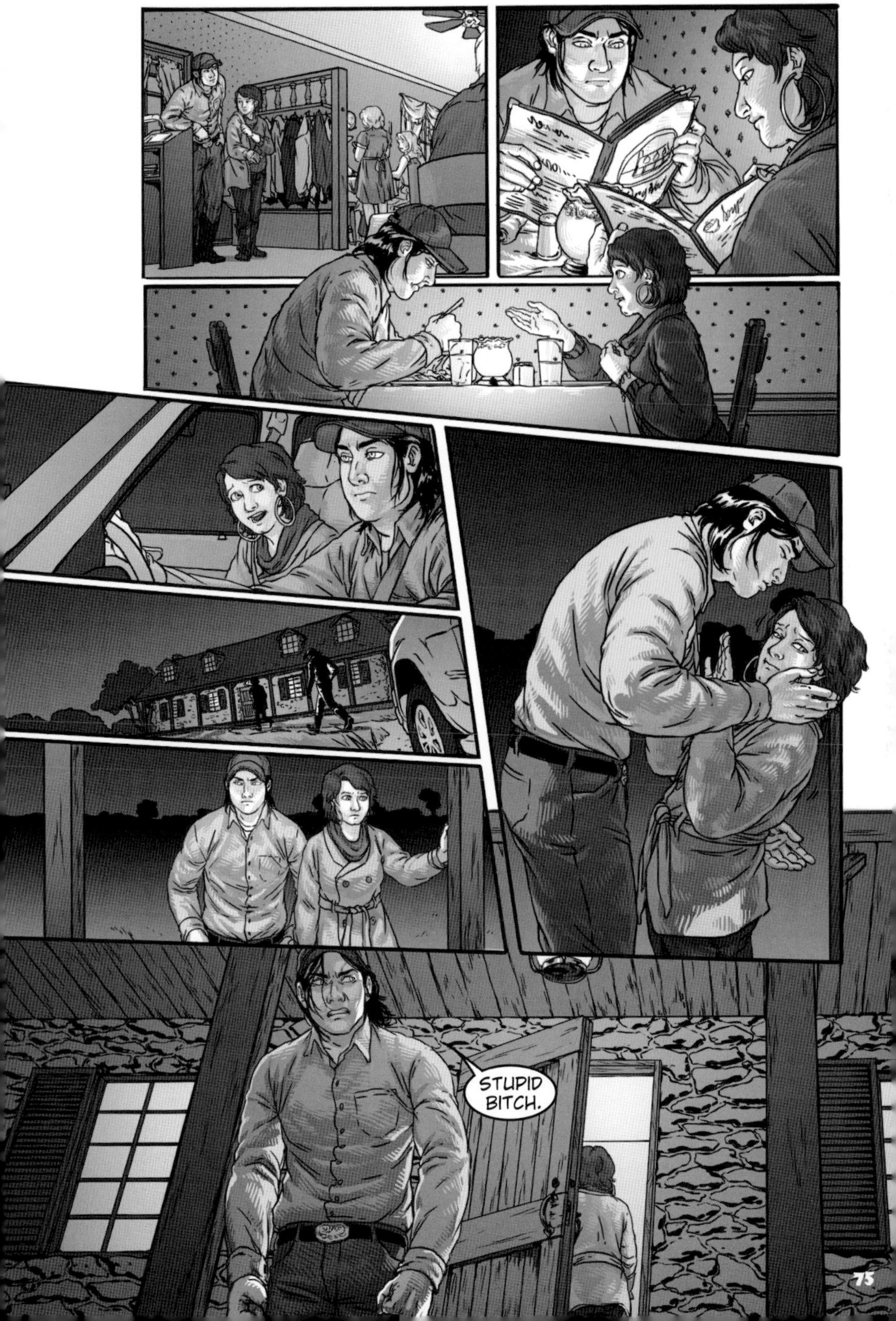
STUPID BITCH.

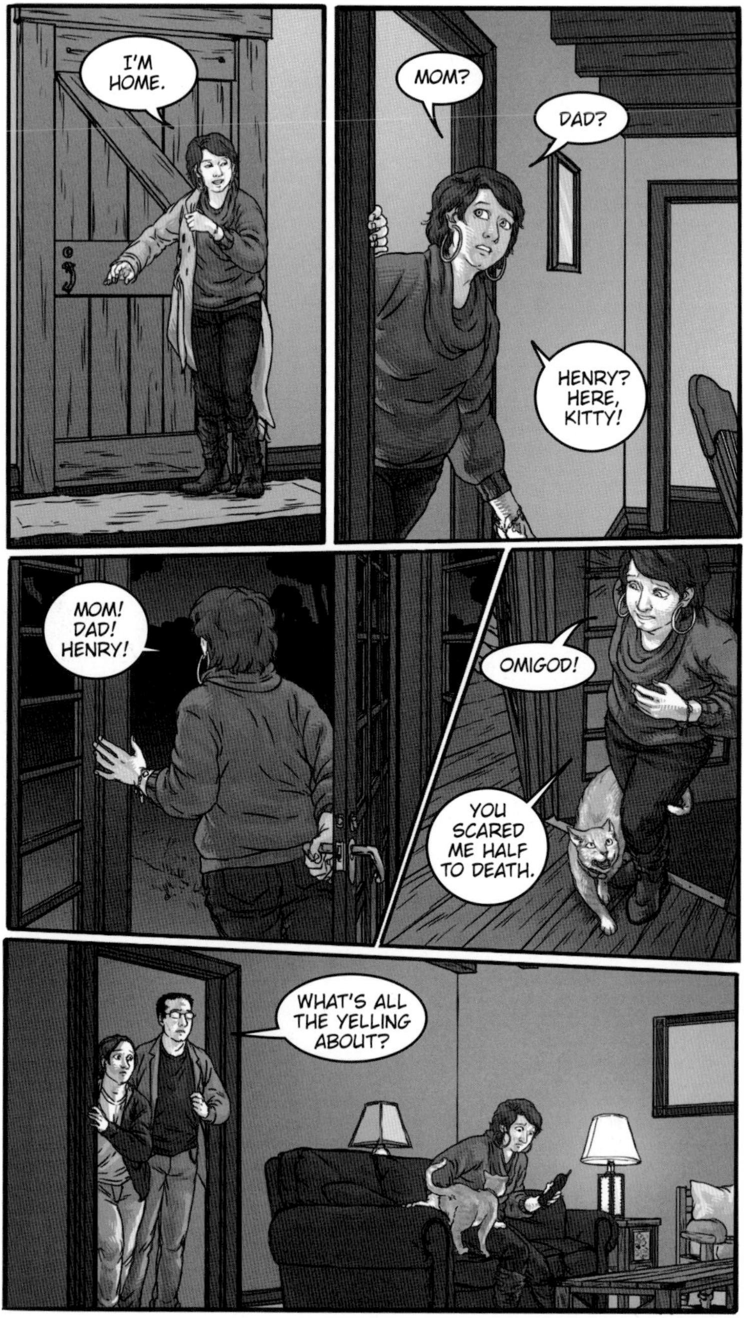
I'M HOME.
MOM?
DAD?
HENRY? HERE, KITTY!
MOM! DAD! HENRY!
OMIGOD!
YOU SCARED ME HALF TO DEATH.
WHAT'S ALL THE YELLING ABOUT?

77

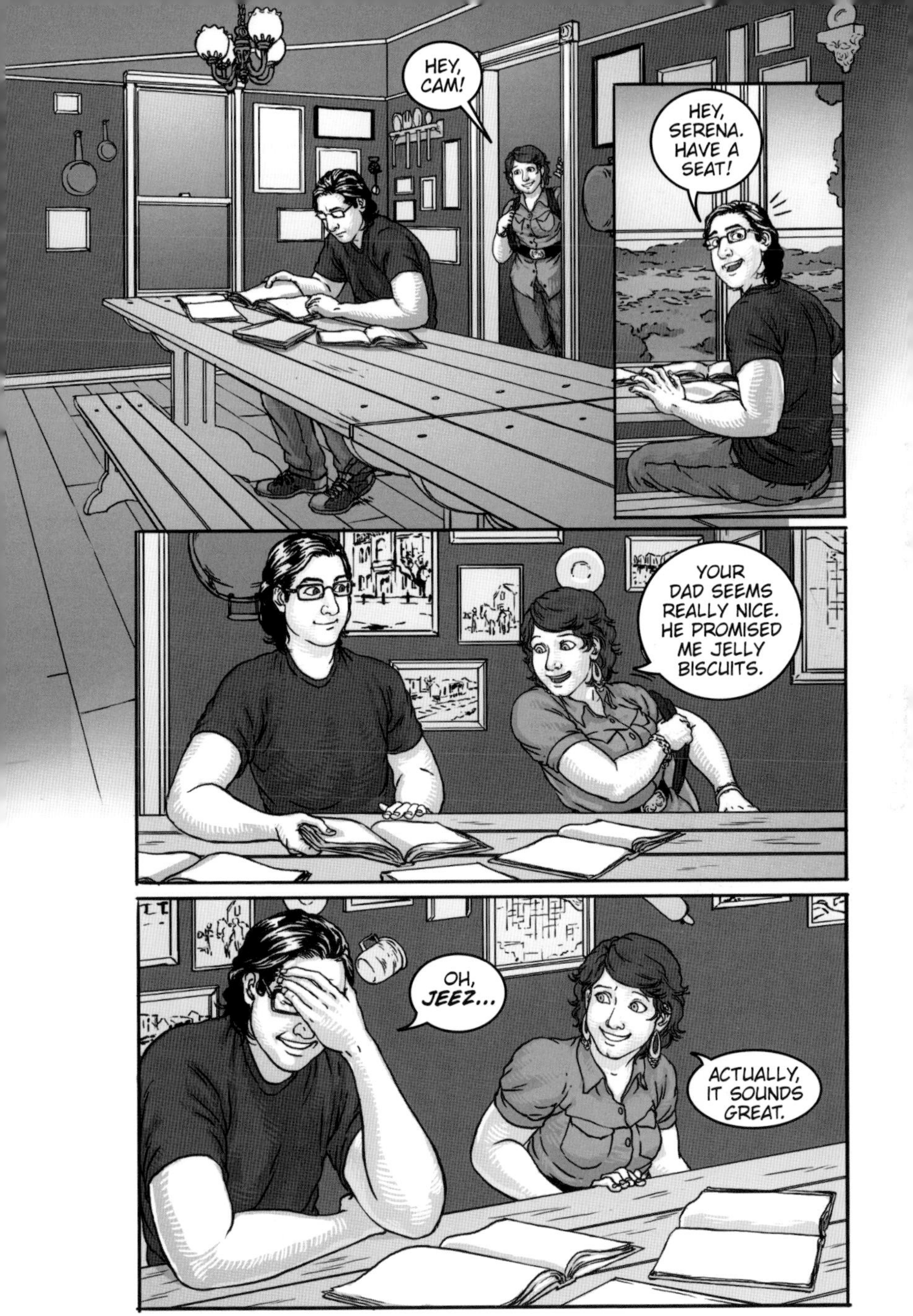
HEY, CAM!
HEY, SERENA. HAVE A SEAT!
YOUR DAD SEEMS REALLY NICE. HE PROMISED ME JELLY BISCUITS.
OH, JEEZ...
ACTUALLY, IT SOUNDS GREAT.

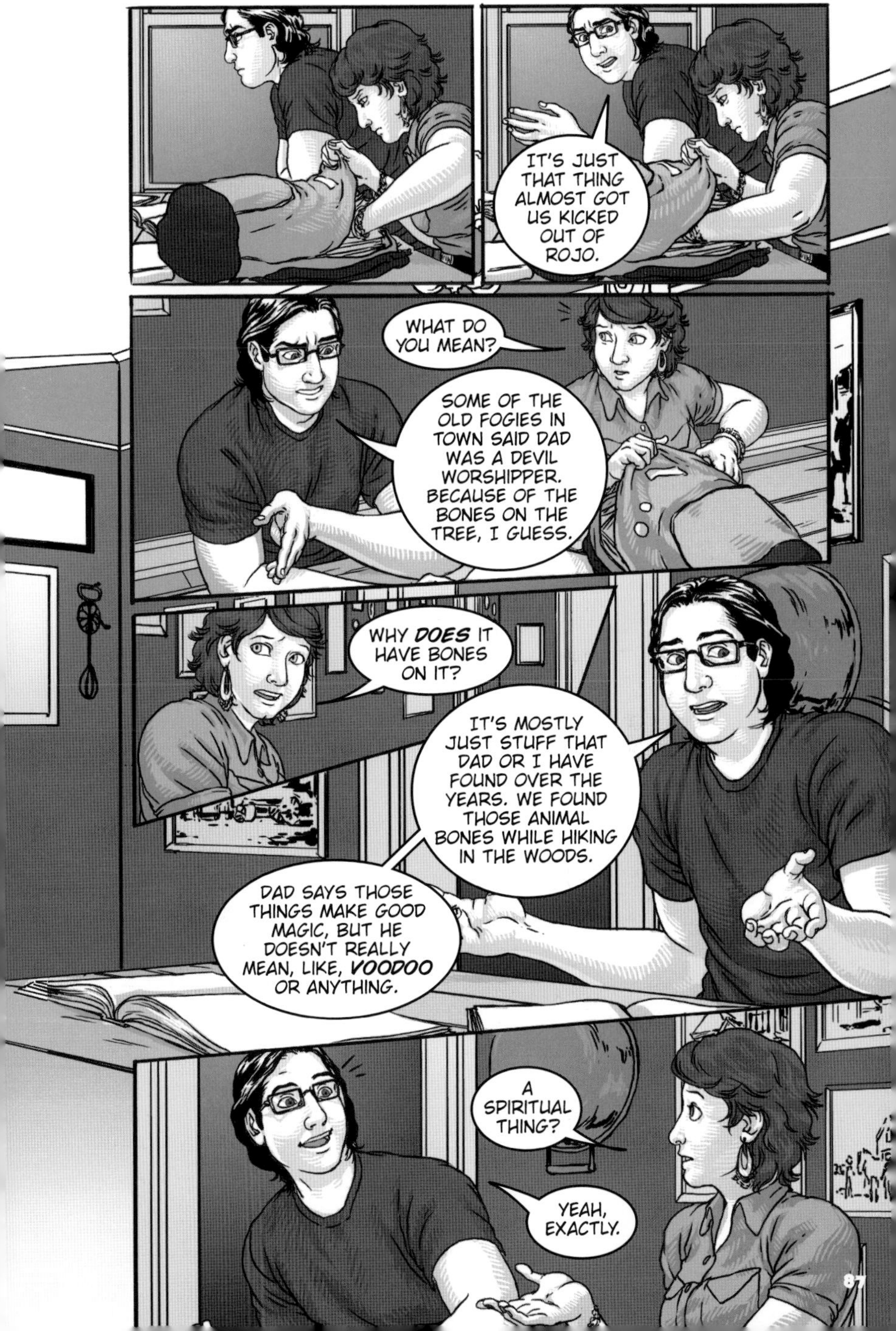
IT'S JUST THAT THING ALMOST GOT US KICKED OUT OF ROJO.
WHAT DO YOU MEAN?
SOME OF THE OLD FOGIES IN TOWN SAID DAD WAS A DEVIL WORSHIPPER. BECAUSE OF THE BONES ON THE TREE, I GUESS.
WHY ***DOES*** IT HAVE BONES ON IT?
IT'S MOSTLY JUST STUFF THAT DAD OR I HAVE FOUND OVER THE YEARS. WE FOUND THOSE ANIMAL BONES WHILE HIKING IN THE WOODS.
DAD SAYS THOSE THINGS MAKE GOOD MAGIC, BUT HE DOESN'T REALLY MEAN, LIKE, ***VOODOO*** OR ANYTHING.
A SPIRITUAL THING?
YEAH, EXACTLY.

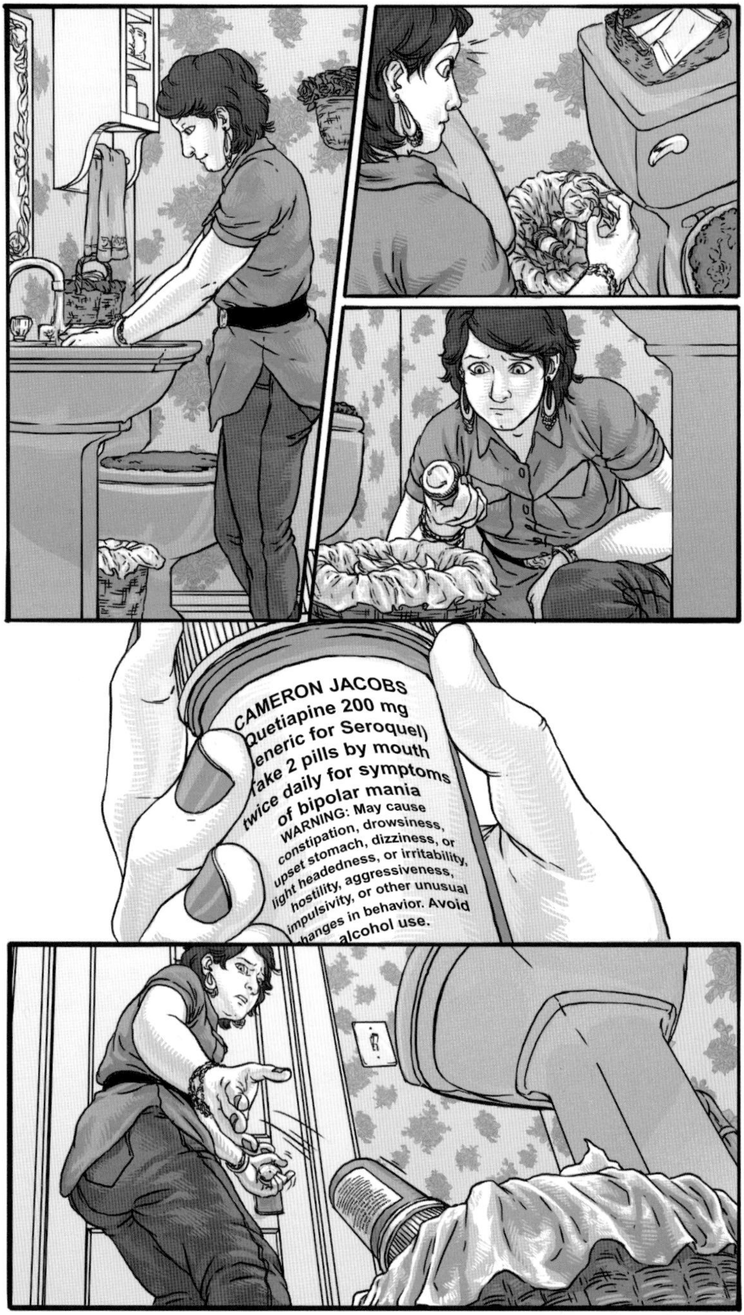
CAMERON JACOBS
Quetiapine 200 mg
eneric for Seroquel)
ake 2 pills by mouth
twice daily for symptoms
of bipolar mania
WARNING: May cause
constipation, drowsiness,
upset stomach, dizziness, or
light headedness, or irritability,
hostility, aggressiveness,
impulsivity, or other unusual
hanges in behavior. Avoid
alcohol use.

91

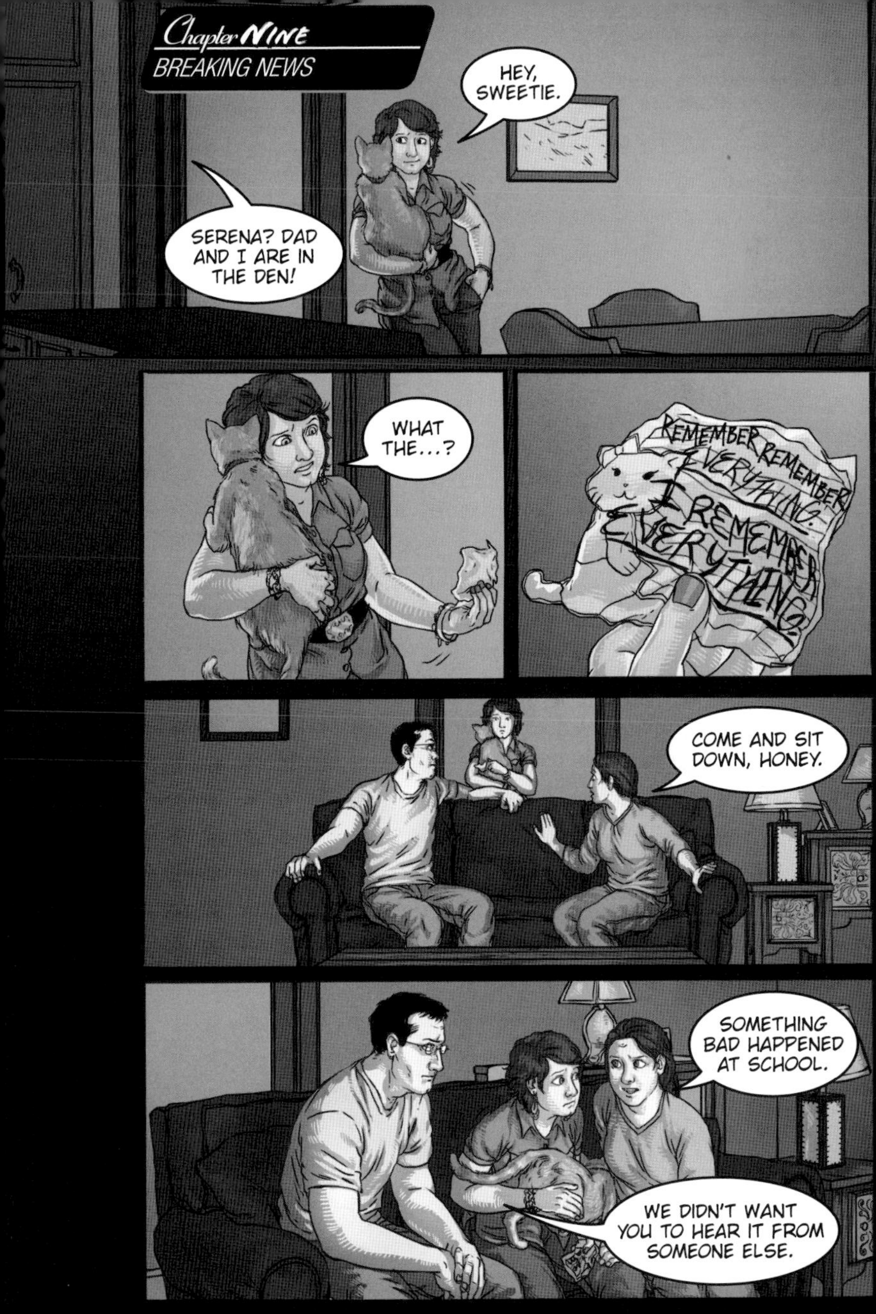
Chapter NINE
BREAKING NEWS
HEY, SWEETIE.
SERENA? DAD AND I ARE IN THE DEN!
WHAT THE...?
REMEMBER REMEMBER EVERYTHING. I REMEMBER EVERYTHING.
COME AND SIT DOWN, HONEY.
SOMETHING BAD HAPPENED AT SCHOOL.
WE DIDN'T WANT YOU TO HEAR IT FROM SOMEONE ELSE.

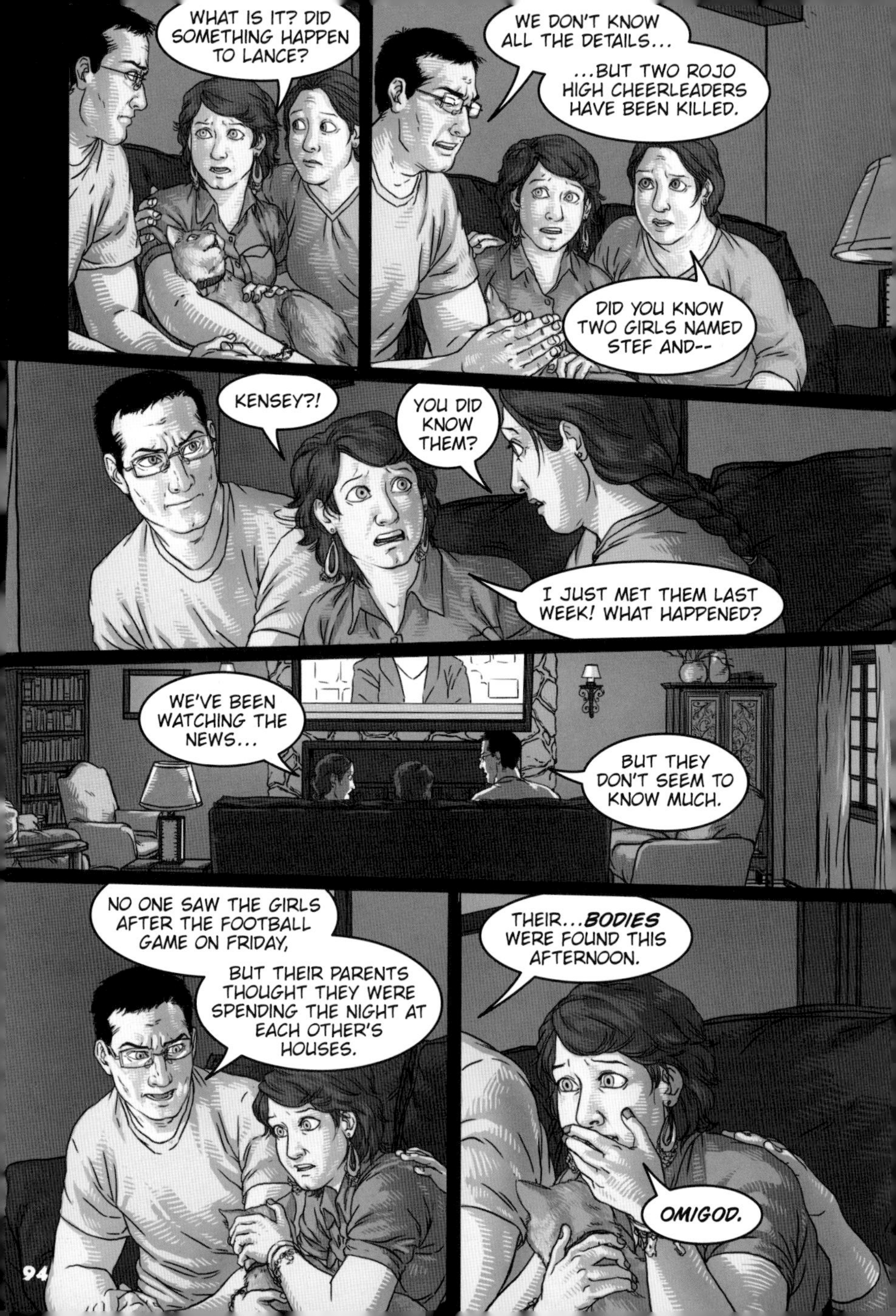

WHAT IS IT? DID SOMETHING HAPPEN TO LANCE?
WE DON'T KNOW ALL THE DETAILS...
...BUT TWO ROJO HIGH CHEERLEADERS HAVE BEEN KILLED.
DID YOU KNOW TWO GIRLS NAMED STEF AND--
KENSEY?!
YOU DID KNOW THEM?
I JUST MET THEM LAST WEEK! WHAT HAPPENED?
WE'VE BEEN WATCHING THE NEWS...
BUT THEY DON'T SEEM TO KNOW MUCH.
NO ONE SAW THE GIRLS AFTER THE FOOTBALL GAME ON FRIDAY,
BUT THEIR PARENTS THOUGHT THEY WERE SPENDING THE NIGHT AT EACH OTHER'S HOUSES.
THEIR...*BODIES* WERE FOUND THIS AFTERNOON.
OMIGOD.

95

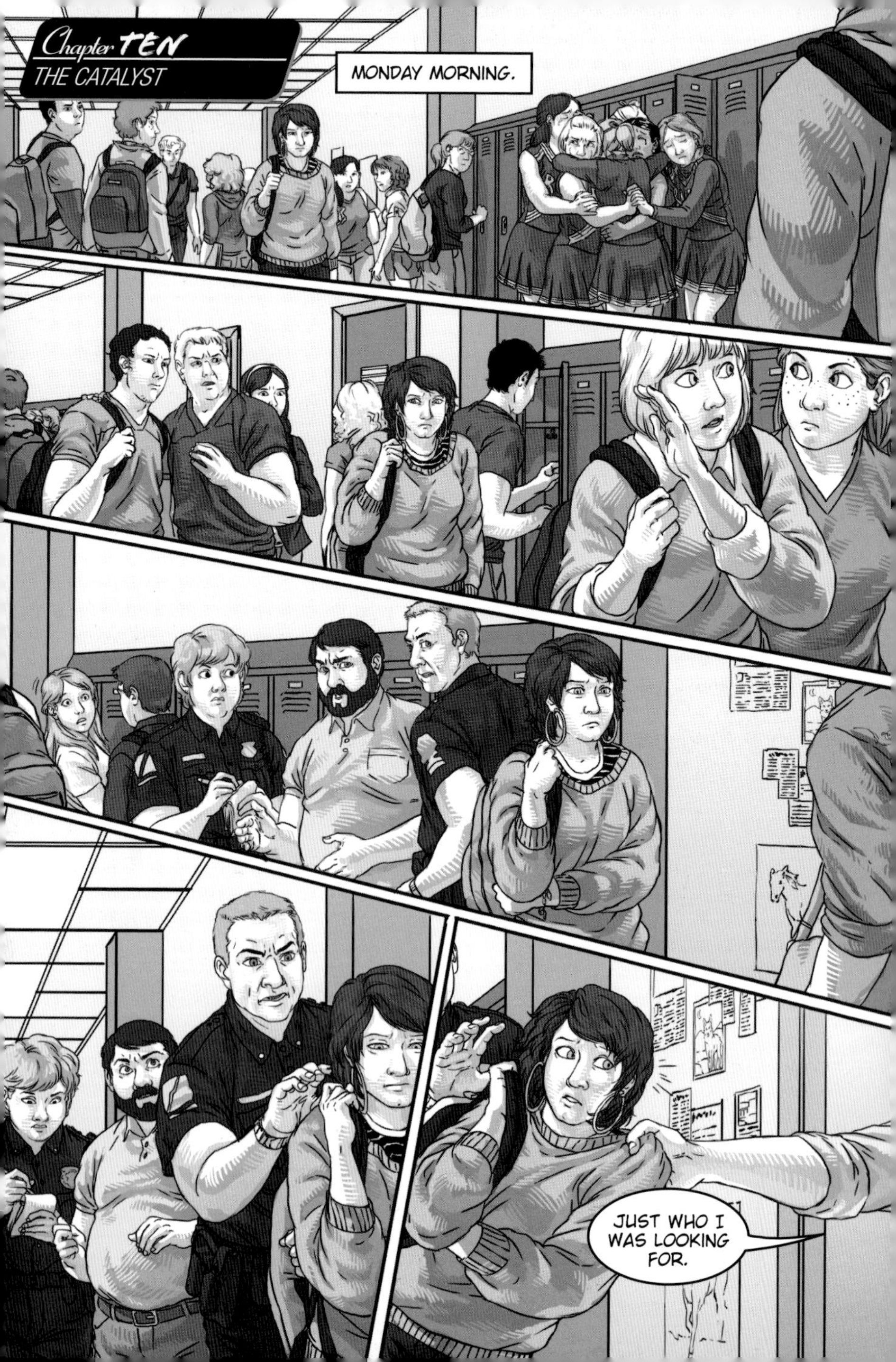
Chapter TEN
THE CATALYST
MONDAY MORNING.
JUST WHO I WAS LOOKING FOR.

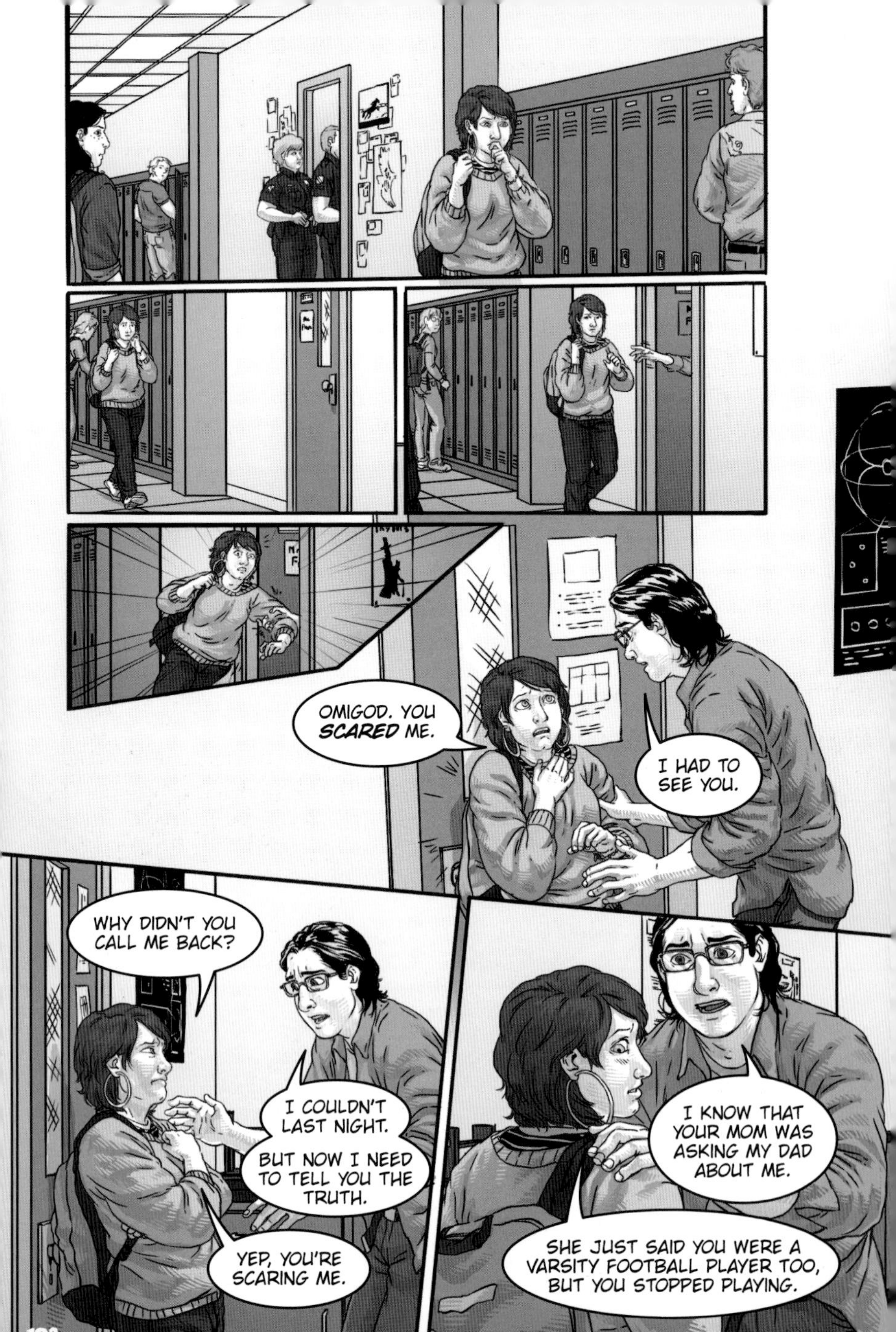
OMIGOD. YOU *SCARED* ME.
I HAD TO SEE YOU.
WHY DIDN'T YOU CALL ME BACK?
I COULDN'T LAST NIGHT.
BUT NOW I NEED TO TELL YOU THE TRUTH.
YEP, YOU'RE SCARING ME.
I KNOW THAT YOUR MOM WAS ASKING MY DAD ABOUT ME.
SHE JUST SAID YOU WERE A VARSITY FOOTBALL PLAYER TOO, BUT YOU STOPPED PLAYING.

I HOPE NOTHING. I JUST GOT HOME, AND THEY AREN'T HERE.

A TEACHER DROVE ME HOME. HE--UM, KNOWS ABOUT THE SITUATION.

I *DOUBT* IT!

EDWARD FOUND OUT SOME REALLY SCARY STUFF ABOUT LANCE AND CAM!

LANCE HAS A RECORD AS LONG AS MY ARM.

LIKE, THEY'VE BOTH CHANGED SCHOOLS A BUNCH OF TIMES IN THE PAST COUPLE OF YEARS...

GUYS... I KNOW THAT. I--

LANCE RACKED UP ALL KINDS OF VIOLATIONS IN FOOTBALL.

HE'S BEAT UP OTHER PLAYERS ON THE FIELD, IN THE LOCKER ROOM--

I--

EDWARD HAS A THEORY.

HE FOUND OUT ALL THIS VIOLENCE STARTED WHEN CAM AND LANCE BOTH GOT TO HIGH SCHOOL.

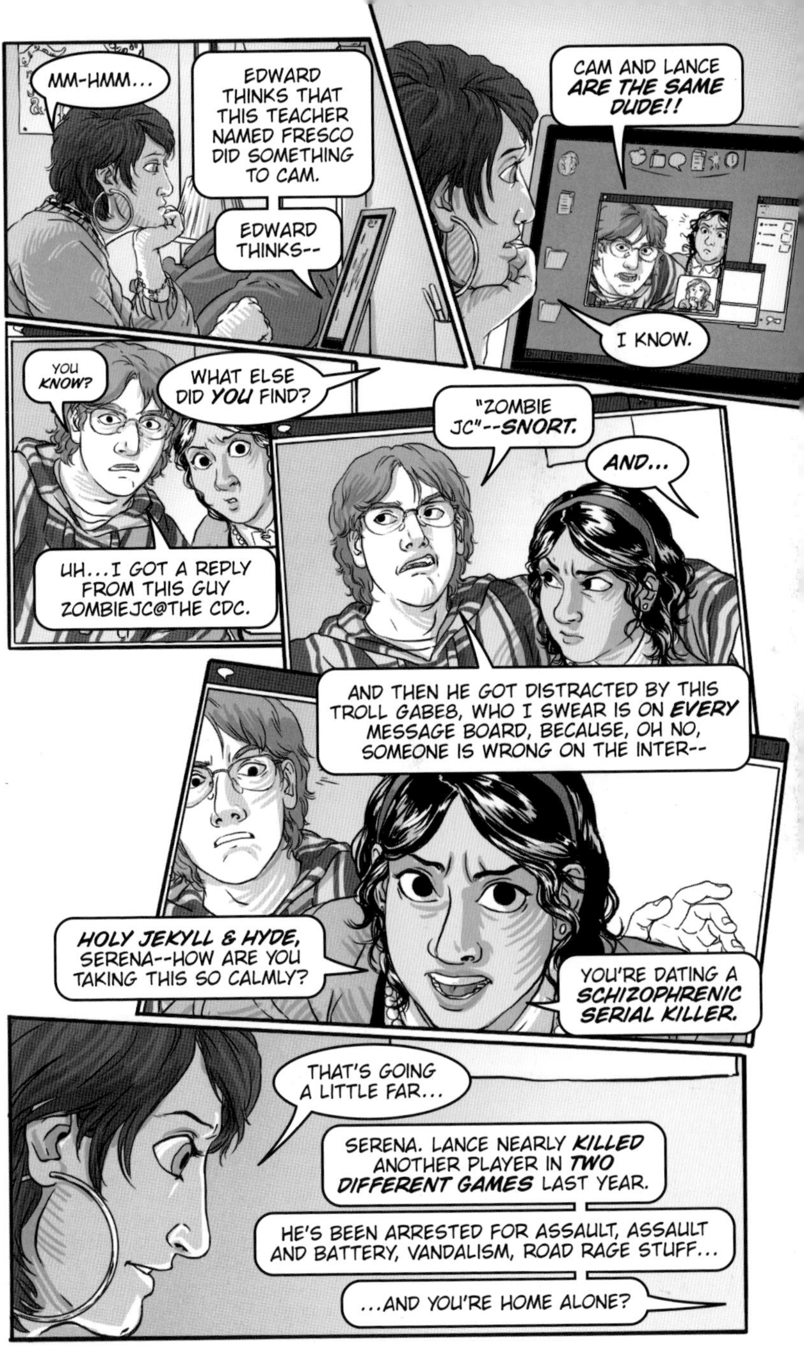
MM-HMM...
EDWARD THINKS THAT THIS TEACHER NAMED FRESCO DID SOMETHING TO CAM.
EDWARD THINKS--
CAM AND LANCE ARE THE SAME DUDE!!
I KNOW.
YOU KNOW?
WHAT ELSE DID YOU FIND?
UH...I GOT A REPLY FROM THIS GUY ZOMBIEJC@THE CDC.
"ZOMBIE JC"--SNORT.
AND...
AND THEN HE GOT DISTRACTED BY THIS TROLL GABE8, WHO I SWEAR IS ON EVERY MESSAGE BOARD, BECAUSE, OH NO, SOMEONE IS WRONG ON THE INTER--
HOLY JEKYLL & HYDE, SERENA--HOW ARE YOU TAKING THIS SO CALMLY?
YOU'RE DATING A SCHIZOPHRENIC SERIAL KILLER.
THAT'S GOING A LITTLE FAR...
SERENA. LANCE NEARLY KILLED ANOTHER PLAYER IN TWO DIFFERENT GAMES LAST YEAR.
HE'S BEEN ARRESTED FOR ASSAULT, ASSAULT AND BATTERY, VANDALISM, ROAD RAGE STUFF...
...AND YOU'RE HOME ALONE?

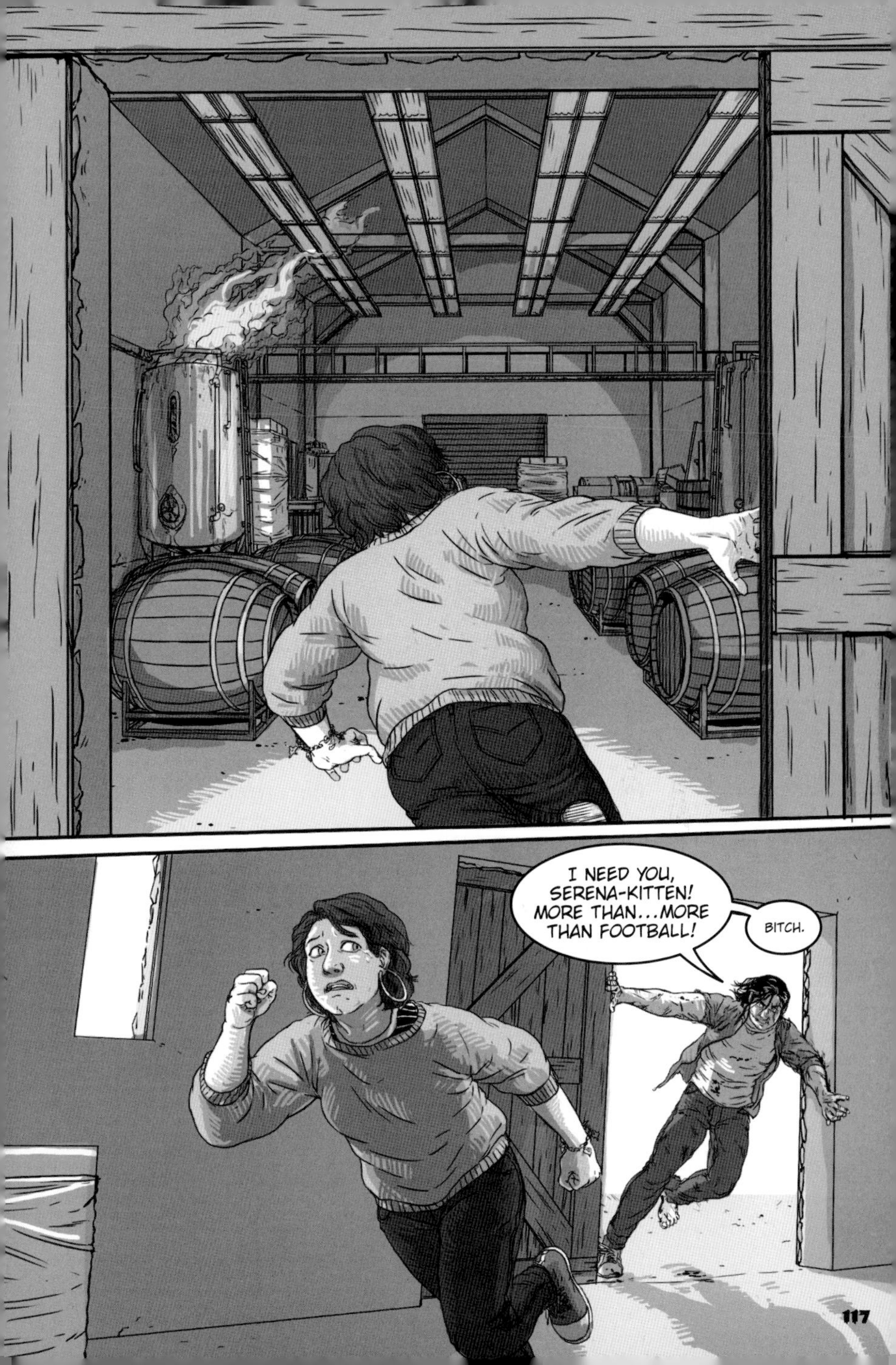
I NEED YOU, SERENA-KITTEN! MORE THAN...MORE THAN FOOTBALL!
BITCH.

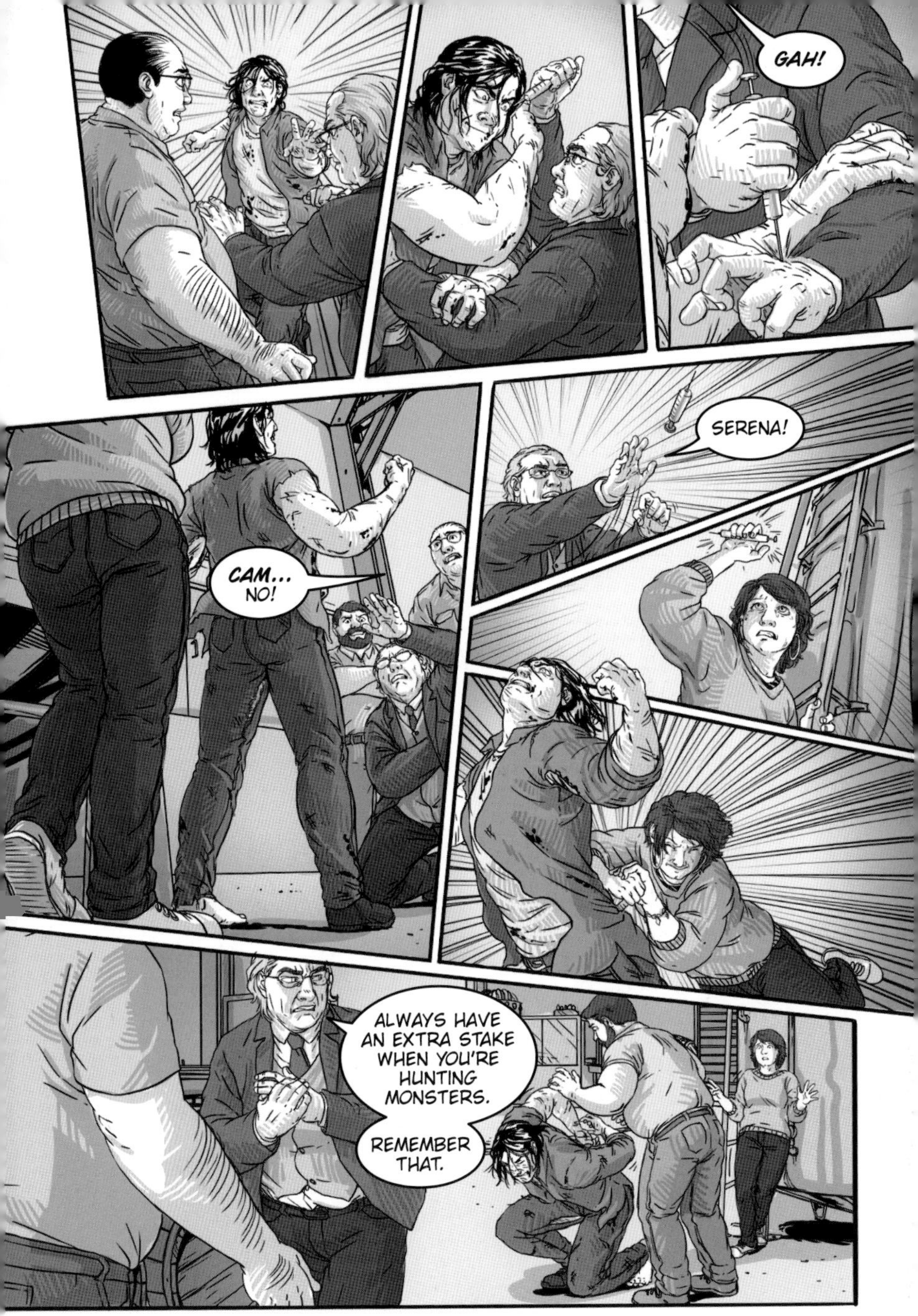
GAH!
CAM... NO!
SERENA!
ALWAYS HAVE AN EXTRA STAKE WHEN YOU'RE HUNTING MONSTERS.
REMEMBER THAT.

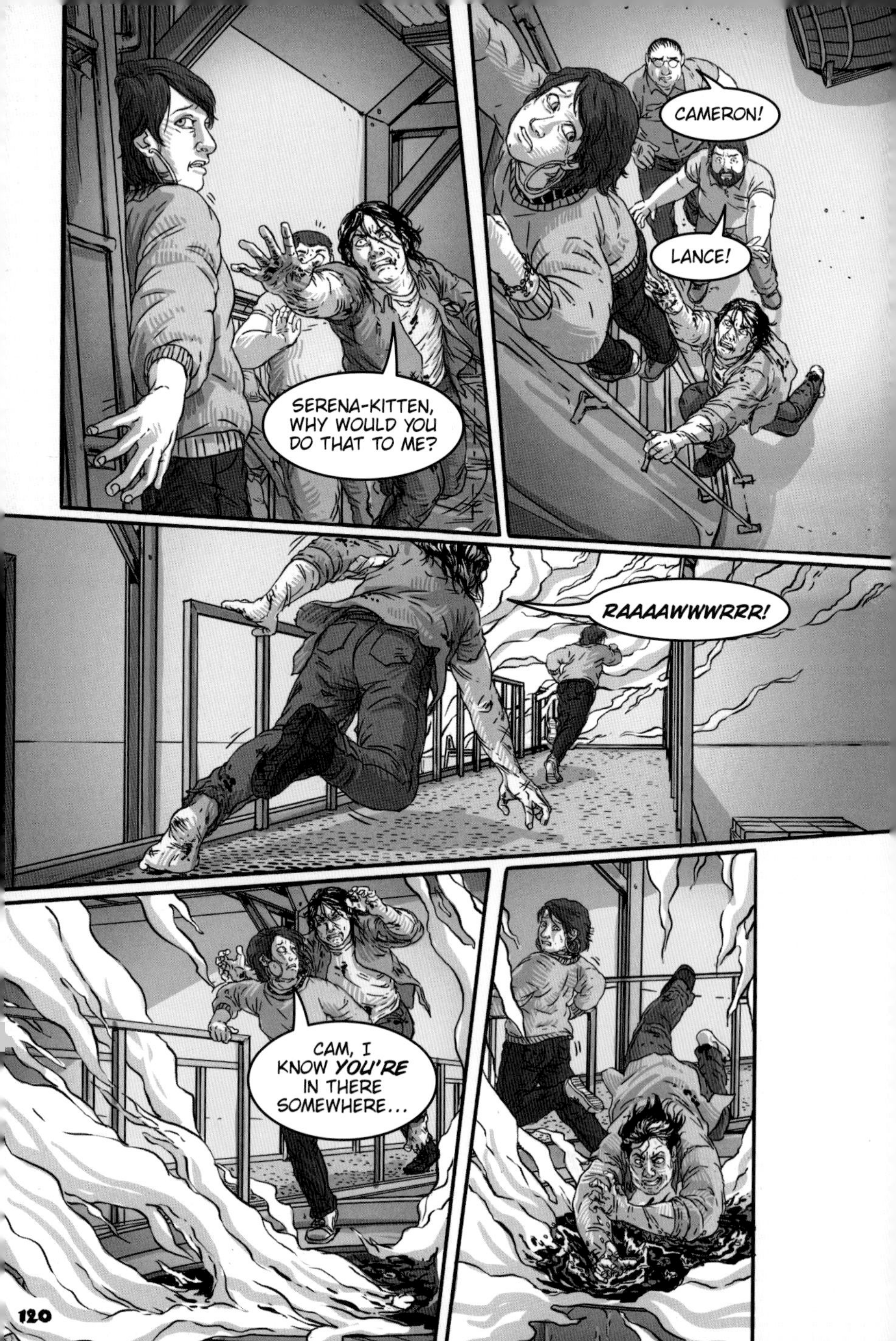
SERENA-KITTEN, WHY WOULD YOU DO THAT TO ME?
CAMERON!
LANCE!
RAAAAWWWRRR!
CAM, I KNOW *YOU'RE* IN THERE SOMEWHERE...

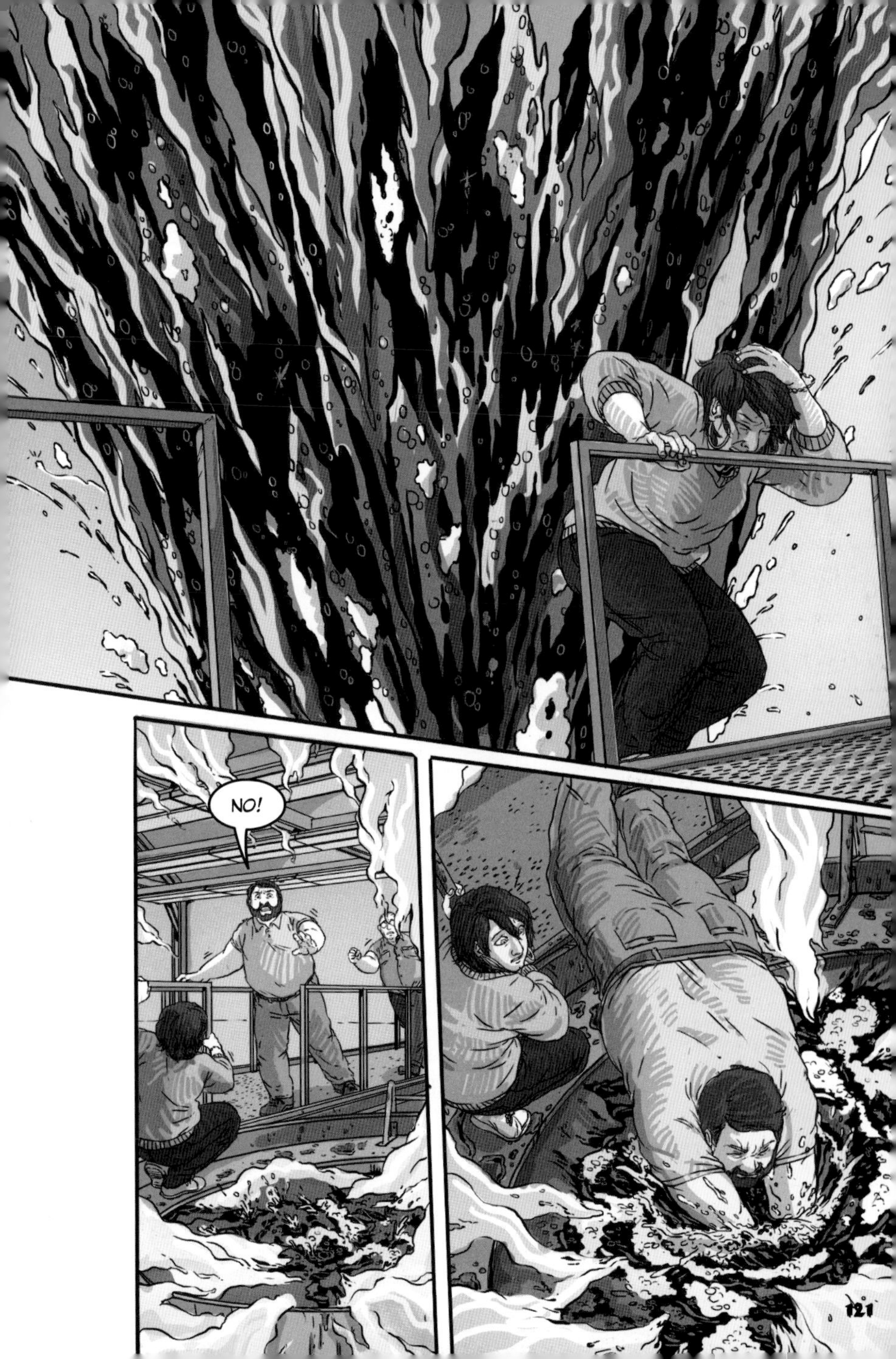
NO!

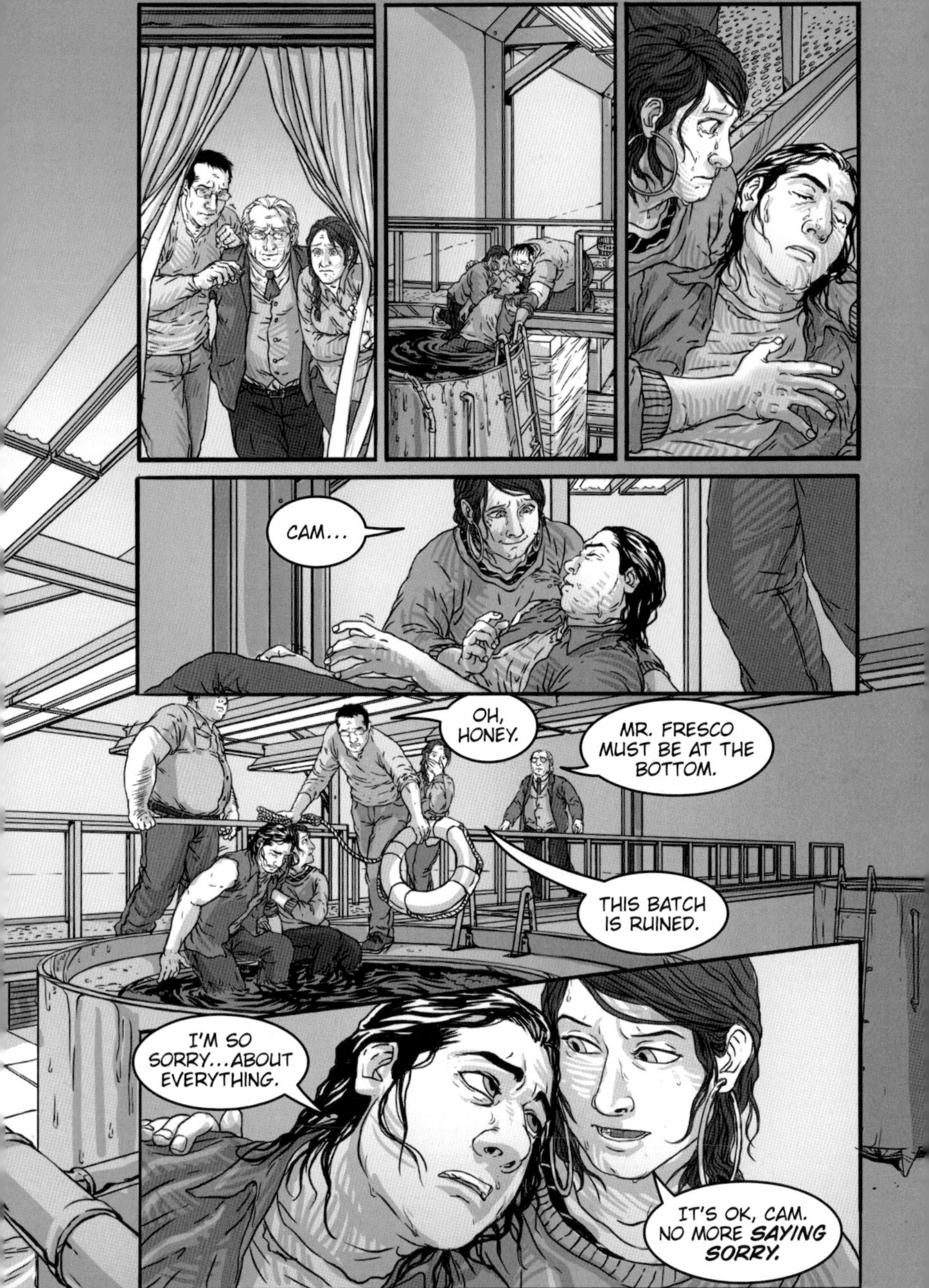
CAM...
OH, HONEY.
MR. FRESCO MUST BE AT THE BOTTOM.
THIS BATCH IS RUINED.
I'M SO SORRY...ABOUT EVERYTHING.
IT'S OK, CAM. NO MORE SAYING SORRY.

SO NO ONE'S GOING TO BE OUT HERE?

NO. CAM'S DAD TOOK HIM TO THIS REHAB PLACE IN PENNSYLVANIA.

MR. BARRY RECOMMENDED IT. IT'S RUN BY THE GOVERNMENT OR SOMETHING.

I THOUGHT CAM WAS CURED BY THE WINE.

HAS SCHOOL BEEN TOTALLY WEIRD?

A FEW PEOPLE LOOK AT ME FUNNY.

VANNS RAILROAD HOTEL EST. 1901

ALL I KNOW IS THAT HE'S UNDER OBSERVATION.

BUT MOST OF THEM ARE FOCUSED ON THE CHEERLEADERS.

THERE WAS A CANDLELIGHT VIGIL FOR KENSEY AND STEF.

LANCE IS STILL CONSIDERED MISSING.

HE'S WANTED FOR THE MURDERS.

ARE THE POLICE LOOKING FOR HIM?

YEAH, BUT THEY DON'T HAVE ANY CLUES.

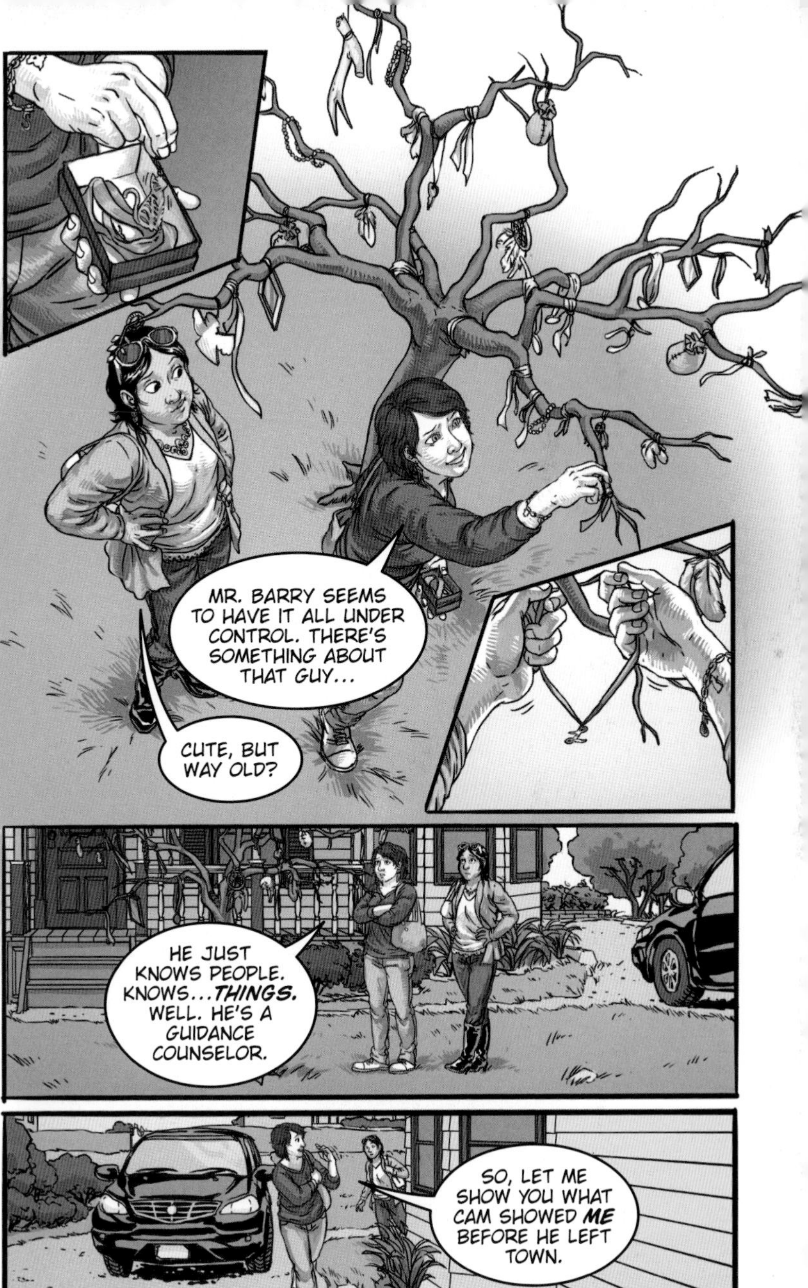
MR. BARRY SEEMS TO HAVE IT ALL UNDER CONTROL. THERE'S SOMETHING ABOUT THAT GUY...
CUTE, BUT WAY OLD?
HE JUST KNOWS PEOPLE. KNOWS...*THINGS.* WELL. HE'S A GUIDANCE COUNSELOR.
SO, LET ME SHOW YOU WHAT CAM SHOWED *ME* BEFORE HE LEFT TOWN.

Class Favorites

Delete!

Francisco Javier "Frank" Fresco
Mr. Fresco is already one of our fave teachers. He's known to wear jeans sometimes, he grades easy, and he brings homemade guacamole to class.

Delete!

Lance Hyland
Most Likely to Succeed—Male
Rojo's star quarterback is our class favorite by a landslide. With that hair, those eyes, and that arm, he could go all! the! way! to the NFL.
Favorites: The Dallas Cowboys, old-school country music, paranormal movies, driving to Austin for a Chuychanga after the game.

Move this to tribute page?

Kensey Hamilton
Most Likely to Succeed—Female
She's a cheerleader, she's pretty—and she's super nice. Clearly, she's going places.
Favorites: North Star Mall, musicals, cheerleading, and her Pomeranian, Peeta. (We don't judge.)

Quinn J. James
Not everyone can get away with wearing wing tip shoes, but Mr. James pulls it off. Our top hats are off to you, Mr. James.

y
s
bout to
logical
like he
in the
student.
make
elieve!"

Serena Stevens
Most Likely to Date Your Boyfriend She may be new here, but she's already dating our starting quarterback, and rumor puts her with Cameron Jacobs as well. Girls, lock up your guys!
Favorites: Cats, turquoise jewelry, cats, English literature...and did we mention cats?

Cameron Jacobs
Most Mysterious
Does Cameron actually go to school here? Or does he just show up in the chem lab every often to set girls' hearts on fir Your guess is as good as ours we're guessing he's going to a Nobel Prize one day.
Favorites: We have no idea Serena Stevens...oh yeah, w went there!

The Rojo High
Reflections

ABOUT THE AUTHOR AND THE ARTISTS

ROBIN MAYHALL has been writing since she could hold a pen. She is a corporate communications writer by day and a published speculative fiction poet and fantasy author. An honors graduate of the University of Texas at Austin with a bachelor's degree in journalism, she lives in Louisiana with three cats who only occasionally attempt to sit on her keyboard. Her previous title for Graphic Universe is Twisted Journeys #16, *The Quest for Dragon Mountain.*

KRISTEN CELLA hasn't gotten out much—out of Illinois, that is. She was born in Chicagoland, grew up in the suburbs, graduated from Northern Illinois University in 2009, and has no plans of quitting the state anytime soon. While she has a multitude of interests that have come and gone and come again, including playing soccer and the violin, her love for art and stories has always stayed constant. She indulges both of these through her webcomic *Antagonist,* which can be found at antagonist.swimtrunkstudio.com.

DIRK I. TIEDE, creator of the manga series *Paradigm Shift,* has been posting comics online since 1999. His artwork was featured in Season 3 of NBC's *Heroes.* His website is dirktiede.com.

JANE IRWIN is the creator of *Vögelein,* an independent comic book, and the *Clockwork Game* weekly webcomic about the world's first chess-playing automaton. Her website is vogelein.com.

JENN MANLEY LEE was a founding member of the Stumptown Comics Foundation and works as a graphic designer. She keeps the home she shares with spouse Kip Manley and daughter Taran full of books, geeks, art, cats, and music.